Murder at the Library

by
Ed Folino

Murder at the Library x2
by Ed Folino
Copyright © 2015 Ed Folino

ISBN 978-1-63360-012-6
For Worldwide Distribution
Printed in the U.S.A.

When I went through my brain cells for a location for this murder, I thought back to my childhood in Pittsburgh, Pennsylvania. Across from my grade school, St. Catherine's of Sienna, was a synagogue. It had large pillars and was quite an impressive structure for its day in the 1950's. I was never inside this synagogue, so any description of the inside of it is purely drawn from my imagination.

Chapter I

I hate Monday mornings. Especially when they are cold and snowy. I was in a deep sleep when my alarm clock went off at seven. I could hear the noise of the salt trucks as they treated the streets. I don't hear them that often since they typically show up around noon. When I looked out my bedroom window, there appeared to be about four or five inches of new snow on the ground. I guess I should expect this kind of nasty weather living in Claysville, Illinois.

My name is Pete Petrone and I'm a Detective Sergeant with the Claysville Police Department. I live with my father, in his home. He was recently diagnosed with dementia. He is not too bad now, but the doctors have told me he will get worse. That's the funny thing about this disease: there is no cure, you never get better, and you only get worse.

I've been divorced now for two years. I lived in an apartment with my ex-wife until my father was diagnosed. She didn't want to move in with him because she felt she had a lot more living to do and didn't want to spend it living with an invalid and a man who was married to his work. Those comments, and a great many more, were the major causes for our divorce. My ex-wife and I were close to forty when we married. After eighteen years, I was left with nothing. When I sit down and think about our marriage, I can't even recall many good memories. I guess it's just my father and I now. At least for the time being I can still have a decent conversation with him.

I had just put my Father's cereal on the table when the telephone rang. It was the station's secretary, Joy, and she said that she'd just received a forwarded 911 call. The caller's name was Rena Renton. Miss Renton was a librarian at

1

the Claysville Public Library. On the 911 call, she reported finding a body when she arrived at work.

I asked Joy who was available to assist me on this call. "I'm sorry, the only detective available is Tim Johnson," she informed me.

Tim Johnson was a recently promoted Detective. He had been on the force for only a few years and everyone knows that he received his promotion because he is the Mayor's nephew. He is a nice enough kind of guy, but seemed a little short in the brains department. I would go on this call by myself, but the department rules stated that murder investigations were to be investigated by two detectives. I told Joy to put Tim on the line because I wanted to speak to him.

"Hello Pete. A murder investigation, huh? My Uncle said it has been fifteen years since a murder was committed in Claysville; I'm looking forward to it."

"So am I," I said to myself in a sarcastic kind of way.

I told Tim that I would meet him at the library in about a half hour and for him not to go into the library until I arrived. Knowing Tim's reputation, I didn't want to get this investigation started on a sour note by him talking to someone before I did.

I finished setting up my Father's breakfast and told him what was available for lunch. I asked if there was anything else I could get for him. "I'll be fine for the rest of the day." He reminded me that I promised to take him to the Claysville Senior Center the following day to play bingo with his men and lady friends.

I told him that I had remembered. It's a shame seeing this man lose his independence. It seems like I do everything but go to the bathroom for him, and believe me I would if I had to. I told him I would call sometime in the afternoon to see how he was doing. I turned the page in the TV guide to Monday, December 10th. All my Father did most of the day to occupy his time was eat, watch TV, and frequent the bathroom. I thought to myself, "I wish there was more to his life than this."

Chapter II

Claysville is a small town located about forty miles outside of Chicago. There are two colleges there: a community college and a campus for the Illinois State University. Around forty years ago, Claysville was a booming steel town with seven or eight large steel mills operating at once. It has now been reduced to one mill and a few steel fabricating plants. The largest fabricating plant is the "Claysville Fabricating Works." Everyone just calls it, "The Works." A great deal of our steel making skills were stolen by the Japanese. However, whatever "The Works" does has not been duplicated by them, yet.

Thank God I drive a Jeep. Even though the streets have been salted, they are still slippery in spots. What a way to start the day. Heavy snow, temperatures in the teens, and a murder investigation with Tim Johnson. It's going to be a long one.

On the way to the library, I observed several college kids on their way to school. I couldn't believe how some of them were dressed. Shorts and t-shirts and it was sixteen degrees outside. Is this the way they show up for class? I know nobody really gets dressed up anymore, but some of the outfits they were wearing were ridiculous—ah, the future of America. I'm glad I'm fifty-eight years old now. I don't want to see what some of them will look like when they finally do grow up.

Chapter III

I met Tim in front of the library and I couldn't believe he listened to me. This was a good start. "Hi Pete, I have an important question for you," he said as soon as he saw me.

"Here we go," I thought to myself.

Tim said, "Let me know when I can go out and get a bite to eat. I rushed out of the house this morning and I haven't had any breakfast yet."

I told Tim as soon as we see what happened here he could go get something to eat. If this was an important question, I can't wait until he had a stupid one.

The Claysville library was housed in a huge building. Back in the fifties it was a synagogue. The massive white pillars in the entranceway are long gone, having been replaced by two large glass doors. The library is located in a residential section of Claysville. There is a ranch style home located to the right of the library, and to the left a home that must be over a hundred years old.

The front door of the library was locked. I tapped my keys on the glass. In a few moments an attractive woman answered the door. She opened it and introduced herself after we identified ourselves, "My name is Rena Renton."

I said, "Is it Miss or Mrs. Renton?

"It's Mrs. Renton, but please call me Rena."

When Tim and I entered the library, Rena said, "I have been the head librarian here for the past eight years." From that introduction, I gathered that Tim and I were supposed to be impressed with her title and position. Rena confirmed she was the person who discovered the body, and reported finding the body at ten minutes to nine when she came in to work.

"The 911 report was logged in at 9:15 AM. Why did it take you twenty-five minutes to make the 911 call?"

Rena explained that she had a few morning duties around the library to attend to before she made the call.

What could be more important than calling and reporting that you found a dead body in the library? In fact, how did you know he was even dead?"

"Oh, he's dead all right," Rena replied.

I was getting ahead of myself since I hadn't seen the body yet. Rena was leading Tim and I toward the body when I saw a man sitting at a huge desk. He was crying and I asked Rena who he was.

"That's what I have been trying to tell you. When I discovered the body of Jamie Jamison on the floor I called Jim, I mean Mr. Jamison, immediately. The body on the floor over there is Jamie Jamison, his son."

I told Mr. Jamison that I was sorry for the loss of his son, and that we would speak to him in a few moments since Tim and I needed to check out the crime scene first.

We found the body of a young man in his late teens or early twenties. I couldn't get over the resemblance of the victim to his father. He looked like his father would have twenty years ago. There was a large pool of blood surrounding the victim's head and he was lying face up in it. A few feet from his head was a bloodied piece of red brick. There was no wound on the front of the victim's head, so I assumed he was struck from behind. But, why was the victim lying on his back? I also assumed the victim was turned over so someone could check his pulse to confirm his demise. The coroner and the forensics team were on their way, so I figured I would know more then.

I looked around for Tim and saw he was talking to Rena. I thought he was asking her something pertaining to the case. As I got closer I heard him ask Rena if there was a restaurant nearby that served a good breakfast. I told Tim to go and get some breakfast, but to hurry back before the forensics team showed up.

The library's employees were beginning to arrive for work and I told Rena to send them home and close the library until further notice and that we would contact them later, or possibly tomorrow.

The coroner and forensics team arrived and Tim had returned as well. It was time to talk to Rena and Mr. Jamison. I told Tim to stay with the coroner and to take thorough notes.

Mr. Jamison was still visibly upset, and rightfully so. Rena seemed unusually cool and collected, despite having found a dead body in her library. That was her wording, "*her*" library. I told Mr. Jamison that I could speak to him the following day if he didn't feel like it now, and I asked if he was able to drive himself home. He said that his daughter and her boyfriend were on the way to pick him up. Again, I offered my condolences. I asked Rena to stay at her desk while the coroner and his team investigated the crime scene. I had investigating to do as well.

A couple of the drawers in Rena's desk appeared to be pried open and I asked if they were like that when she left the library on Saturday night.

"The drawers were not like that when I left Saturday night. They were recently replaced a few months ago after a robbery attempt. Now I'll need to have them replaced again." I didn't recall hearing about a break-in at the library, so I made a note to check on that to get the details about the incident.

I asked Rena to tell me everything that happened leading up to the discovery of the body.

"I arrived at ten minutes to nine in the morning, as I always do, and I heard the floor buffer running," she began.

I stopped her. "The machine wasn't running when Tim and I arrived. Did you turn it off?"

Rena said, "Yes, I turned it off because it was getting on my nerves."

I asked Rena if she touched anything else in the library this morning.

She replied, "Just the telephone to call Mr. Jamison and 911. Oh, I also pulled the back door closed. It looks as though that it was pried open."

I went to the back door to see for myself. When I opened the door I observed a recently shoveled walk. It had snowed the night before and I wondered who might have shoveled. I went back and asked Rena if she had done so.

Rena replied, "I have a young man who lives next door and does odd jobs for the library, but he always asks before he does work around here. His name is Patrick Ponzetti. Also, Patrick couldn't have shoveled the rear walk because the back door requires a key and he does not have one."

I wondered if our killer was worried about someone falling on the snow covered walk, or just covering up footprints that were in the snow. I thought I better check with the coroner and see if he had any more information for me. I couldn't rely solely on Tim.

The coroner determined that the victim was murdered between midnight and the early hours of the morning. He elaborated, "The victim died from a blow to the rear of his skull. The killer got lucky here. They hit just the right spot in the back of the head, possibly by chance or possibly by some knowledge of the body. I would say death was most likely instantaneous. I will know more when I get the body back to my lab. I had one of my men bag the bloody section of red brick. I'm assuming that it is the murder weapon."

I questioned the coroner about the position of the body when it was found and shared with him my theory regarding Jamie being struck on the back of the head.

"That is correct, yes," he said.

I asked him, "Then why do you think the victim was

lying on his back? It would seem to me if he was struck on the back of his head the body would have fallen forward." I mentioned that neither Rena nor Jim Jamison had moved Jamie. They both informed me they merely checked the victim's pulse to see if he was dead.

"The murderer may have turned the body over to check the victim's pulse," he replied.

I asked the coroner to call me when he had the final results of his autopsy.

When I went outside, I stood in the front of the library, and a few homeless people passed by. Could one of them have broken into the library looking for food, or maybe looking for something of value to sell? A broken section of a brick could certainly be a homeless person's weapon of choice. There were also a lot of people from the local college walking near the library. I don't think they would chance a criminal record just to steal some books. A college student might have broken in to steal a laptop, but would that be worth killing someone? I saw quite a few computers still located around the library. It was too early to think about suspects too much since the library employees and the victim's family still had to be questioned.

I'd forgotten about Tim. When I caught up to him he said that he was going to get something to eat for lunch.

"What a load I have to carry. Why me?" I thought to myself again.

Some people refer to me as a super cop, and my nickname at the station is "Columbo." I always get my man, or my woman. I was having a bad feeling about Rena Renton, but as I'd said before, it's much too early in the investigation to think too narrowly about suspects.

Jim Jamison's daughter arrived at the library with her boyfriend. This girl was quite the mess! Her boyfriend wasn't any prize either. I didn't know that hippies still existed. I knew that there were kids that looked like hippies, but I didn't know what they called them now. I figured that "Rejects from Society" would be an appropriate name for these two as that's what these two looked like: rejects.

Mr. Jamison introduced me to his daughter and her boyfriend. His daughter's name was Julie, and her boyfriend's name was Buster, an appropriate name for this loser. Julie's hair looked like it hadn't been washed in a few weeks. Her jeans looked even dirtier than her hair. She wore a loose fitting T-shirt that read, "I do drugs." This looked like a truthful statement. Buster's jeans looked as though they were going to fall down any minute. He had a T-shirt that read, "I'm with stupid." This also looked like a truthful statement. It seemed as though these two were inebriated by drugs or alcohol, or both. Jim Jamison looked like a somewhat normal guy. I felt sorry for him. He seemed to be embarrassed by these two.

I asked Julie if she and her boyfriend were able to drive. One of them had to drive their own car, and the other one had to drive Jim Jamison's car.

Julie gave me a resentful stare and said, "Why do you ask, old man?"

"Ah, yes. Class and respect," I thought to myself. I asked Julie where she and Buster had been.

"Buster and I were out most of the night hitting the clubs in Chi-town. I received a call from Rena and couldn't figure out why that slut would be calling me."

I said, "Hold on, Miss. Regardless of how you feel about Mrs. Renton, you should still show her a little respect."

Surprisingly, Julie said, "Oh, the Mrs. Renton who's screwing my Dad." Julie looked at her Dad and said, "Come on Pops, we are so out of here."

I told Julie, Jim and Buster to stay close to home for when I needed to talk to all three of them further. I was going to have my partner Tim question Rena, but after what Julie said, I decided to question her myself. I told

Tim to question the neighbors on both sides of the library, especially Patrick, the kid who did the odd jobs. Someone may have seen or heard something unusual Saturday night or Sunday morning, so naturally we would want to question everyone. Tim said that he would get right on that after he got some lunch. If I remembered correctly, he had just came back from breakfast.

Chapter IV

Tim knocked on the door of the house to the right of the library. Rena told us that a family of four lived there, Mr. and Mrs. John Harris and their two teenage daughters.

The Harris' lived in a well maintained ranch style home. It appeared to be recently painted and the roof looked to be new. There was a snow blower in the front yard. The yard was adjacent to the front sidewalk. Tim assumed the neighborhood was pretty safe since the snow blower was in plain sight and could have been stolen at any time.

Mr. Harris answered the door. He was a tall, thin gentleman who appeared to be in his sixties. Tim glanced around the interior of the home. The furniture all seemed to be new or very slightly used. Tim knew that Mr. Harris' furniture had nothing to do with this case so he erased it from his memory.

Tim introduced himself to Mr. Harris and told him he was investigating a murder at the library.

Mr. Harris acted surprised. "Murder; I knew someone died over there last night, but I didn't know that they were murdered. I don't think we've ever had a murder committed in this neighborhood."

Tim asked Mr. Harris if he or his wife heard or saw anything unusual the night before.

Mr. Harris told Tim, "There was a noise that kept my wife and me awake most of the night."

Tim asked what kind of noise he thought it was, and if he remembered what time it was when he heard it.

"It sounded like a motor running. It started around midnight and didn't stop until around nine this morning. I wondered why a motor would be running that long. I know that there are maintenance people working there at night. I was going to go over and see what was going on, but my wife talked me out of it. She told me I would probably scare the hell out of anyone who may have been there. She also said that whoever was there working probably wouldn't hear me knocking over the noise anyway."

Tim asked Mr. Harris if his wife or children were at home so he could speak to them. Mr. Harris told Tim that his wife went to Sunday Mass and that his two daughters were currently living on campus at Illinois State University. He said that paying for his daughters to live on campus was expensive, but it kept them out of he and his wife's hair, which made it worth the money.

Tim told Mr. Harris that he might have more questions for him at a later date. Mr. Harris said he wasn't going anywhere since he was retired and spent most of his days and nights at home.

As Tim was about to leave the Harris' home, he asked Mr. Harris about the piece of machinery in the front yard. "I assume this is a very safe neighborhood, otherwise why would you leave an expensive machine in your front yard out in the open like that," Tim said.

Mr. Harris replied, "Oh, you mean the snow blower; that's the third one I've purchased this year. Someone keeps stealing them but it's too heavy to haul in and out of my shed each time it snows."

Tim thought to himself, "So much for the safe neighborhood theory."

Tim went to the house to the left of the library next. Rena had told him that the Ponzetti family lived there, with their son Patrick. The Ponzettis' lived in an old frame house. There were artificial rose bushes decorating the front yard. Tim grinned and wondered to himself, "Maybe there's an artificial vegetable garden in the back yard."

Mr. Ponzetti answered the door. He was a short, Italian

looking man who appeared to be in his seventies. He wore wide purple suspenders, which held up his old looking khaki trousers. He had on a white undershirt which had numerous red stains on it. Tim assumed that the stains were probably old spaghetti sauce and held back laughter at that thought.

Tim introduced himself and Mr. Ponzetti told him to call him Mario. Then Mario asked Tim if he would like a glass of homemade wine or a dish of pasta. Tim passed on the wine, but said that he would love a plate of pasta.

Tim looked around the Ponzetti home. The furniture there looked as if it may have belonged to Mr. Ponzetti's father or grandfather. It seemed very old, but also seemed well maintained.

Mario noticed Tim looking at the furniture and said, "Most of the furniture in my home belonged to my wife's parents. This was their home, and after they died we moved into this place."

Tim thought it would be a nice gesture to mention the artificial rose bushes in the front yard.

When he did, Mario said, "My wife makes me junk up the yard every winter with that plastic crap. I cut my real rose bushes down every year and she makes me put that stuff out there because she misses the real ones. Please come back this summer when my real roses are in bloom. They're beautiful."

Just then a huge boy walked into the kitchen. Tim figured that he weighed about 250 pounds and was in his late teens or early twenties. He assumed that it was Mario's son, Patrick. After saying hello to Tim, Patrick told his father that he was going into the living room to watch cartoons. Tim felt that there was something strange about this boy, but couldn't put his finger on it.

Tim and Mario finished their pasta, and he told Mario he had questions for him, his wife, and Patrick.

Mario said, "You can question me, but you'll have to talk to my wife about speaking to Patrick. She's with our neighbor Louise Harris at Sunday Mass. She should be home in a few moments."

Tim said that he had already talked to Louise's husband John. Tim asked Mario if he knew about the murder at the library, or if he had seen or heard anything unusual from the library last night.

Mario said, "Yes, I've heard about the murder. I heard the sound of a motor coming from the library that started around midnight. I couldn't recall what time it stopped. My wife and I watched TV until 2:30. When we went to bed we could still hear the noise. When we woke up at nine this morning the sound was gone."

Just then Mario's wife came home. She was your typical looking Italian homemaker and was wearing a pretty cream colored dress, and a huge flowered red hat. She wore nylons that must have been a few sizes too large as they were rolling down her legs.

Mario said to his wife, "This is Detective Tim Johnson from the Claysville Police Department. He's here to ask questions about the murder at the library last night. He needs to question both of us, and I told him everything that I know. I don't think you'll have anything to add. Oh, by the way, he wants to question Patrick, too and I told him he had to wait for you to get home before he could question him."

Tim told Mrs. Ponzetti that her pasta was delicious and that he had a nice conversation with Mario. Tim told Mrs. Ponzetti that Mario asked him to call him by his first name. Tim asked Mrs. Ponzetti what her first name was.

She said, "My name is Mrs. Ponzetti. I don't think you'll have to talk to my son. I'm sure Mr. Ponzetti has told you everything that we know. Now if you don't mind I have to get my dinner started."

Tim was going to ask Mrs. Ponzetti if he could take some pasta with him, but he nixed that idea after she seemed upset with him.

Chapter V

Tim came back to the library to tell me how his questioning went. I asked if any of the neighbors saw or heard anything unusual last night. He reported that neither of the neighbors told him they saw anything unusual, but both families said that they heard some kind of noise that seemed like a motor. I asked Tim if he talked to the kid who did odd jobs around the library.

Tim said, "The mother wouldn't let me talk to the kid. There's something strange about him. He's probably around twenty years old and he has to be home by seven every night. He goes to bed at ten every night, and apparently he still watches cartoons on TV."

I told Tim that watching cartoons was not that strange, and that I still watched them once in a while. I also told him that we could talk to Rena about the boy because she's the one who gave him the odd jobs.

Tim said, "Rena, huh? Are you two on a first name basis now?"

I said, "Don't worry about it, and it isn't really any of your business."

Sometimes that Tim really got on my nerves. I told him I was going to question *Mrs. Renton* some more and asked if he knew that Jim Jamison and Mrs. Renton were having an affair. Tim asked me how I knew that already and I told him that it was something Jim Jamison's daughter informed me about. Tim said that he was going down the road to get a snack. The poor guy was hungry. He has had a rough day so far.

Rena was sitting at her desk and I realized that I was getting hungry. Tim must be rubbing off on me. I asked

Rena if she wanted to go out and get a bite so we could get better acquainted. She told me of a small restaurant/lounge right down the street from the library called Max's. She said that they served huge sandwiches that were out of this world. I thought to myself, "I wonder if Tim has found this restaurant yet? Am I stupid? Of course he has."

I wasn't surprised when I saw Tim sitting at the bar as Rena and I entered Max's. I was hoping that he wouldn't spot Rena and I, but he looked at me with a huge smirk on his face and said loudly, "Hello Peter."

"Hello Tim. It sure is funny finding you here."

He couldn't respond because his mouth was full.

Max's was a small sports-orientated lounge/restaurant. There were tables surrounding a horseshoe bar. There were photos of Chicago sports figures adorning most of the wall space. I'm not much of a sports enthusiast so these photos did nothing for me. There were small poker machines every four or five feet at the bar. I assume they were put there for the many college students that frequent the establishment. The bar area was very dark.

Rena asked if I wanted to eat at the bar or sit in the dining room. I told her that I wanted to be as far away from Tim as possible, so the dining room would be great. We were seated at a small table in the rear of the dining room which was also very dark. I don't know if the owner was saving money on lighting or if he was providing indiscreet couples a dark place to hide.

Rena asked the waitress what the soup of the day was. She replied that wedding and bean were both available. My mother used to make great wedding soup. I've tried a few at the local restaurants in Claysville, but none of them came close to my mother's. Bean soup was out of the question. I never ate bean soup when I was out, only at home, so I thought I'd chance the wedding soup. Rita selected the wedding soup as well. While we were waiting for our soup we looked over the menu. I've never seen such a large selection of sandwiches.

Rena told me that "Max's Cholesterol Overload" sandwich was probably the most popular so I figured I'd try that, and double up on my Lipitor pills when I got home. Rena said that she was going to order the same.

Rena was an attractive woman in her mid forties. I say in her mid forties, but she could have been thirty or sixty because I am very bad at determining a person's age. Rena had long red hair and carried a beautiful body with her. I could see why Jim Jamison may have been attracted to her. Before we left the library, I told Rena that this would be a social lunch, but I decided to get a little background on her.

I began by asking how long she'd worked at the library.

Rena replied, "I've worked in this library system for twenty-eight years. I worked at the main library in Chicago for twenty years, and then I was transferred to the Claysville branch eight years ago. With that transfer, I was promoted to the Claysville library's head librarian."

Although I didn't see a wedding ring on Rena I asked her if she was married. Rena replied, "I have been married to my husband Ed for twenty six years, but that doesn't mean I'm a one man woman. We have two beautiful daughters who are twelve and sixteen." I didn't know exactly what that statement meant, but it sounded like Rena was coming on to me. She asked me if I was married.

"I have been divorced now for two years," I said. "My wife couldn't have children. We went through twenty years of marriage with two dogs. My wife kept our last dog in the divorce settlement, and as far as a relationship goes, I don't have time for one. All my time is consumed with my work and taking care of my father, who was recently diagnosed with dementia." I figured that would put a little water on that potential fire. All I needed was to get involved with a suspect, if in fact she was one.

Rena asked me how long I've been a detective.

"I've been a policeman for thirty years now, the last nine as a detective. I really enjoy my job. I don't think there's any other work that I would rather do," I replied.

Just then Tim poked his head into the dining room. He said, "I'll see you back at the library Pete." He added, "How about the sandwiches in this place?"

I said, "I don't know, I haven't received mine yet."

Tim said, "Hey, take your time, I'll see you later."

I thought, "Wow, Tim has given me permission to take a long lunch. Wasn't that nice of him?"

Thank God our soup finally arrived. The only problem with that was the sandwiches also arrived at the same time. I decided not to say anything to the waitress as maybe it wasn't her fault.

The soup was excellent. Of course it was not as good as my mother's, but it was close. The sandwich was huge. It contained ham, egg, bacon, sausage, cheese, lettuce and tomato, and a big glob of mayonnaise. The bread appeared to be fried on a grill in butter. It was so big I could hardly get my mouth around it. I knew that I couldn't finish it, so I decided to save half of it and put it in my car. It was cold enough outside, so I knew it would not spoil. I planned on giving the leftover half to my father when I got home.

I looked over at Rena. She didn't appear to be having trouble tackling this monstrosity. She told me when she gets a sandwich at Max's, she only ate a half of it and that she always saved the other half for her husband, Ed.

I figured the small talk was over. It was time to get back to the library and hear Rena's story. And besides that I had to think up something for Tim to do. I told Rena that I was now ready to question her.

Rena seemed a little shocked and said, "What do you mean question me? Am I a suspect?"

"In this business everyone is a suspect until I decide

they aren't." I told her to just answer my questions and I would decide if she had a solid alibi, and if she didn't want to answer my questions now, we could take her to the station to do so.

I told Rena that a solid alibi would be a confirmation of where she was at the time of the murder. I said she would need to have witnesses collaborate that they saw or were with her at the time of the murder. I also told her I would question her husband as well. I asked Rena to account for her time between midnight and six in the morning.

"I was home in my bed. I had watched a Gary Grant film festival on the AMC channel last evening. I watched two movies, *Charade* and *To Catch a Thief,* and then I went to bed around midnight."

I asked Rena if anyone else was at home. She said that her husband was attending a union meeting in Chicago and must have arrived home after she went to sleep, and that her daughters were spending the night with her sister in a small town on the other side of Chicago. She said that they didn't get home until Sunday night.

I told Rena that on a scale of one to ten, her alibi rated at a five. "There aren't any witnesses to tell me if you were home at the time the victim was murdered," I said. I told Rena that there may be one more thing. I decided to be blunt. "Were you and Jim Jamison having an affair?"

Rena told me that she and Jim Jamison sometimes had a few drinks at Max's. She continued, "Jim Jamison is my employee. Jim and his son Jamie worked for me for the last three months. Jim owns a maintenance company that I hired to clean the library. He usually works at the library alone. When I hired him, he told me that his son would help him only if he had to do any work on the library's floors. Jim's son Jamie was with him when I hired him. The next time that I saw Jamie was this morning when I discovered his body."

I asked Rena what days and hours Jim Jamison worked at the library.

"Jim works Tuesdays through Saturdays from eight in the evening until five in the morning. I often worked a few extra hours a couple nights a week, and that is when Jim and I would go out for drinks."

I asked Rena if she went out for drinks with any other of the library's employees.

"It's not what you think. We are just good friends. Jim has had it rough. His wife died of Cirrhosis a few years ago. I know you've met his wacky daughter and her boyfriend, and now his son has been murdered."

I mentioned that I would be questioning Jim Jamison, his daughter, and her boyfriend tomorrow. I then asked Rena how much money was usually kept in her petty cash drawer, and if anything else may have been stolen.

Rena said, "We have twelve laptops in the library and all of them are here. I didn't notice anything missing except for the petty cash. I will check more thoroughly tomorrow morning. As far as the petty cash drawer goes, we normally keep twenty dollars in cash and five dollars in coins. The drawer was empty when I arrived this morning, except for the change. We use the petty cash for making change for fines, and the money is also used to pay our neighbor Patrick for doing the odd jobs around here."

I said, "Oh yeah, that reminds me of another question I wanted to ask you. What's the story on Patrick?"

Rena said, "Patrick is a nice boy. He's just a little slow. His mother had him when she was close to fifty years old. Neither of Patrick's parents will admit that there is anything wrong with him. Patrick is eighteen years old now, but I'd say he has the mentality of an eight to ten year old child. I've created little jobs for Patrick to do around here. The hardest job he may do around here is to shovel the front walk of the library."

I asked Rena if Patrick ever shoveled the rear walk of the library, because I noticed it was shoveled the night of the murder.

Rena replied, "No one ever uses that entrance. It's actually a fire exit." Rena continued, "And besides that, Patrick would never do any work around here until he checked with me. He sort of has a crush on me, you know?"

It was still bothering me that someone shoveled the rear walk. I wondered a lot of things. "Why did they do it? Were they getting rid of their footprints? It has to be someone who knew what they were doing. Where did they get the shovel?" I remember Tim telling me that he looked around and couldn't fine a shovel anywhere in this library.

I asked Rena if the library had a snow shovel and she said that Patrick brought his own shovel from his home. It appeared to me that whoever murdered Jamie drove to the library last night. I figured that not too many homeless people drive cars, and that would probably eliminate them as suspects. I asked Rena what the best time would be to question her husband.   She told me that her husband Ed worked the four to one in the morning shift at the Works and added that he usually leaves the house around three in the afternoon.

I told Rena that I would be at her home to question her husband in the early afternoon after I visited the Jamison's.

My father really enjoyed the "Cholesterol Overload" sandwich from Max's. Thank God he had dementia and not a weak heart. If he had a heart problem and ate that sandwich, he'd be close to death by now. I think I better go to bed early tonight because tomorrow was going to be a long day.

When the alarm rang I remembered it was my father's bingo day at the senior center and I had to drive him. The center had a small van which they used to drive the seniors home. I went into my father's room to wake him up, but he was already dressed and ready to go. He used to look forward to shooting pool and having a few drinks after work, but now the highlight of his week was playing bingo. I skipped giving my father his cereal this morning because they served a light breakfast at the center. I hope I don't have any trouble getting there since it snowed pretty heavily again last night.

To my surprise the roads weren't that bad. It was a wet snow and easy to get traction. As we were driving to the center, my father looked at me and said, "Peter, I really appreciate everything that you do for me. I enjoy the atmosphere at the center, but once a week is plenty. It reminds me a little too much of an old people's home, and I'm thankful that you granted my wish not to be put in one."

I told my father that taking care of him was a sort of a payback for all the years he took care of me.

My father continued, "I just hope I wasn't the cause of your divorce. I can't help thinking that I was the cause of your wife leaving you."

My wife didn't leave me. I left her. But I didn't want to correct my father as it tended to confuse him. I told him that he was not the reason for my divorce and that there were many other reasons which caused it. Actually, he was the reason for my divorce, but it was going to happen sooner or later, really. We arrived at the center and I offered to take him in. He still had a little of independence in him, though. He thanked me, told me he would be fine, and said he would see me that evening. I said a little prayer that he would win a game. It's funny how most people only pray when they want something, and I was one of those people, I guess. After I thought about it, I realized I wasn't asking God for something for me, I was asking for my father.

Well at least Monday was out of the way; let's see what the next day would have in store.

I stopped at Tim's desk and we both had coffee. Tim told me his wife made him a big breakfast. I told him I was very happy for him and asked if he received any unusual news from the library's employees he questioned yesterday.

"I questioned three women who worked for Rena Renton," Tim told me. "They all said she was a tyrant to work for, and that she tried to make every man who came into the library. One woman said that it didn't matter how old they were, either. Celine Selsnick said she was dumped by the Vic's Father when he started fooling around with Rena Renton."

That seemed to confirm what Jim Jamison's daughter said to me. I told Tim that women were notoriously jealous of each other, and if they hated Rena like they told him, they were likely say almost anything.

Chapter VI

Dr. Meenan has been the Claysville County Coroner for the past six years. He only works when he is called, which is seldom, because of the lack of suspicious deaths in our city. Dr. Meenan also is a teacher at the Claysville Community College. He's a nice older gentleman and he knows his stuff.

I asked the Doctor what were his official conclusions concerning Jamie Jamison's murder.

Dr. Meenan said, "We have a nineteen year old male who died from blunt force trauma to the rear of his skull. The weapon used was a half of a standard size red brick. The half of the brick had a protruding point of concrete on it where it was separated. The point on the brick which struck the victim's skull caused his instantaneous death. That is my report on the official cause of death. I want to add that it appears that the victim was turned over after the blow to the head was administered. This would explain why the victim was lying on his back. There were no finger prints on the murder weapon, the red brick. An analysis of the red brick revealed pieces of fabric found in cloth work gloves. These gloves are the type normally found in local steel mills and fabricating plants in the Claysville area."

I thanked Doctor Meenan for his report and asked him if he had any other personal observations.

The Doctor said, "As I told you previously the murderer got lucky. He or she hit one of the softest parts of the victim's skull. The victim died instantly.

I asked the Doctor if the blow could have been administered by a woman or a small person.

He told me it would not take a great deal of force to

administer the deadly blow because of the position on the head where the victim was struck. He confirmed that the fatal blow could have been administered by a person of any size, man or woman.

I told the Doctor that I had a problem with the fibers found on the brick and I asked why there weren't any fibers on the back door or on Rena's desk drawers where the petty cash was kept.

The Doctor said, "It doesn't make any sense to me either. It seems to me that the murderer may have brought two pair of gloves with him, one for breaking into the library, and one for handling the brick. Another scenario would be that the murderer wore one pair of gloves to handle the brick, and he or she didn't care if their prints were found in the library. To me, this scenario would suggest that the murder was committed by someone who works in the library. I know your men searched the library and adjoining grounds, and no red brick sections were found. I assume that the half of red brick was brought to the library to kill Jamie Jamison. My forensics team seems to think that the damaged desk drawers and the forced open rear door were done to make it appear as if there was a robbery attempt. I can tell you this Pete, if you find the other half of the red brick you've probably found your murderer."

I thanked the Doctor for all his information. I asked him one more question. I asked if he could tell me who the murderer was.

The Doctor smiled and said, "I did my job, now it's your turn to do yours. Good luck."

Chapter VII

I decided to call home and check on my Father. It took a while for him to answer the phone. Besides the dementia my father had a severely enlarged prostate. The doctors wanted to remove it, but my father chose not to have the surgery. The medicine he is taking works somewhat but he still urinates frequently every day and into the night.

Well, there was some good news. My father won a bingo game and was so excited. I asked him what he won and he said, "A fifteen dollar gift certificate for some restaurant called Max's." He asked me if I ever heard of the place.

I told him that the half of sandwich I brought him home the night before was from Max's. He said, "That was a huge sandwich and it was good. I'll get one of those and have a half left over for another meal."

I congratulated him on his win and reminded him to take a few pork chops out of the freezer for dinner.

The snow had finally let up. I made my way to Jim Jamison's to conduct some more questioning. He lived in the western part of Claysville. There were many expensive homes in this area of town, and Jim lived in one of them. I think I picked the wrong career. It seemed that office maintenance paid very well. Actually, my definition of office maintenance is that it's a glorified name for a janitor.

Jim Jamison's daughter Julie opened one half of the huge white double door to their home. I couldn't believe my eyes. She looked almost normal and was wearing black slacks and a pretty red blouse. Her hair looked like it may have been shampooed, and it was combed. I wondered if her father had spoken to her about her appearance.

Julie told me that we could talk in her dining room

after I spoke to her father. She said her father was in the living room finalizing plans for Jamie's funeral. I asked Julie where Buster was and she told me that he was out of town.

I was perturbed and said to Julie, "He was not supposed to leave Claysville. I thought he knew that."

Julie said, "Yes, he knew that, but there are no jobs in Claysville and he wanted to check out an opportunity he saw in this mornings newspaper."

I asked Julie to contact Buster and tell him that he had to return so I could question him. Julie asked me if Buster was a suspect, and I told her that everyone is a suspect until their stories are checked out.

Julie said, "There's one thing you should know about Buster. He was only charged with that robbery.

He was never convicted."

I looked at Julie like I knew what she was talking about. I excused myself and called Tim and told him to check out this Buster character for prior arrests. I told him to check out Julie Jamison as well. Tim asked me why he had to do this.

I told him not to worry about it right now and that we would compare notes at the station later.

I thanked Julie for her time and told her I would talk with her further after I spoke to her father.

I couldn't believe how nice this girl could be when she wasn't under the influence of alcohol or drugs.

Julie led me into the living room to meet her father. I re-introduced myself to Jim Jamison and offered my condolences to him once again.

I started my questioning by asking how long his son had worked at the library.

Jim hit me for a loop when he said, "My son's murder was entirely my fault."

I asked Jim what he meant by that remark?

"My son and I stripped the old wax off the library's floors last week. We were almost finished on Friday. The only thing that needed done was to shine the floors with the buffer Saturday night. I was supposed to go to the library Saturday and buff the floors myself, but I told Jamie I wasn't feeling well and Jamie told me he would finish them. If I wasn't feeling so lousy I would have been there instead of him."

I asked Jim what was wrong with him, because he seemed okay to me right now.

Jim continued, "Rena broke up with me on Friday night. I was devastated because I really loved her."

"Wait a minute," I said. "Rena said that you and she only went out for cocktails a few times."

Jim told me that his relationship with Rena started the first night that he worked at the library, and it lasted nearly three months. Jim said that on that night he worked at the library and they went down the road to Max's for a few drinks, and he took her to his apartment.

Jim continued, "I have an apartment on the East Side that I use for sexual encounters. I've had a few non-meaningful relationships that started and ended in that apartment, but my relationship with Rena was different. I really cared for her. I guess she didn't care for me as much as I thought. I got the apartment because I didn't think it was appropriate for me to be doing something like that in my home. After my wife died a few years ago, it didn't seem right having sex with a woman in the same bed where I slept with my wife. And besides that, the kids are still living there. I was falling in love with Rena and I told her that last Friday night. Rena told me that she didn't love me and that she was in our relationship only for the sex. I couldn't believe she had said that to me. I wanted her to get a divorce from her husband, Ed, and marry me. Rena told me that would never happen. I told her that I would give her all day Saturday to think about us and that if she didn't agree to get a divorce, I was going to call her husband Sunday morning and tell him everything."

"I called Rena at her home Sunday morning. She answered and immediately told me that she wouldn't put her husband on the phone. I told her that I'd thought about our affair and decided that she just wasn't worth it, and she didn't have to worry about me saying anything to her husband. Rena was silent for the longest time. I thought she'd hung up".

"I told Rena that I had actually called to ask her if she had heard from Jamie"

Rena said, "No I haven't heard from Jamie." She continued, "Tell me Jim, why didn't you work at the library Saturday night?"

I told Rena that when she told me she didn't love me I became really upset and that I was too depressed to go to work Saturday night, so I sent Jamie to finish the floors. I told Rena that Jamie didn't answer the phone at the library, so I asked her if she could meet me at the library and see what was going on.

Jim said, "Rena agreed to meet me, and that's when we discovered Jamie's body. That's all I have for you, detective."

I thanked Jim for his cooperation and then I went to the dining room to speak to Julie. My cell rang before I went to the dining room and it was Tim. He told me he had some information about Julie's boyfriend, Buster. I said I would call him back because I didn't want Julie to hear me talking about her boyfriend. I told him to call the Ponzetti's and tell them I wanted to question their son, Patrick. I also told Tim to tell them that they could be forced to have their son answer my questions and reminded him to be nice, but firm, to the Ponzetti's.

Chapter VIII

Julie was sitting at a huge glass oval dining table. This thing must have cost a fortune. The six chairs surrounding it weren't too shabby either. I said, "I'll say one thing Julie, you sure do live in a fine looking home, and it is furnished quite well. How can a maintenance man afford a home like this? Did your father hit the lottery?"

Julie said, "First of all, my father owns his own maintenance company, and second of all, yes, he did hit the lottery. My Father won $750,000 off the Illinois lotto game a few years ago. He won the money a short time after my Mother died. Then he purchased this home and furnished it with the finest furniture and accessories he could buy. Does that answer your questions?"

I told Julie I was sorry and that I didn't mean to sound rude. I was just curious.

Julie told me to have a seat, and that she was ready for my questions. She offered me a cup of coffee but I declined. I told Julie that I didn't really have a lot of information about her brother, and could she give me some. I asked her for a list of names and phone numbers of Jamie's friends.

Julie said, "Jamie didn't have a lot of friends. He did have one friend he was very close to. His name is Bruce Banton and I'll give you his address and phone number when we are finished here."

I thanked Julie for the information and said, "I'm sorry I have to ask you this, but where were you between midnight and six o'clock Sunday morning?"

Julie replied, "I don't know if my father told you, but Jamie was my half-brother. My father married my mother when I was six years old and then they had Jamie. My mother had me out of wedlock, and I don't know who my real father is, and I don't care."

I told Julie that I've talked to her and her father and they both had given me shocking news. I asked Julie if she had any more surprises for me.

Julie said, "Jamie was gay, but I wouldn't consider that shocking, would you?"

"I would, if it has anything to do with his murder."

Julie told me Jamie made a play for Buster once, but that she had smoothed over that situation. I kept this little information about Buster and Jamie in my memory. I asked Julie again where she was on the morning of the murder.

Julie said, "I arrived at my house around three in the morning. I was with Buster and we hit the clubs in Chicago Saturday night into Sunday morning."

I asked Julie if anyone else was with her.

She said, "No, and if you're going to ask me the names of the clubs, I can't remember."

I thought Julie's and Buster's alibis were pretty weak. Either one, or both of them, had plenty of time to kill Jamie Jamison.

Jamie added that she had no reason to kill her step-brother.

I told Julie that she may not have had a reason to kill Jamie, but Buster did.

Julie told me that I was making too big a deal about the gay thing with Buster and Jamie. "I'm sorry I mentioned the whole incident," she said.

I told Julie that I was done questioning her for now and told her to get in touch with Buster as soon as she could. I added, "Tell your boyfriend that if he doesn't come back immediately I'll have a warrant issued for his arrest."

Chapter IX

I called Tim and told him to meet me at the station. I was going to question Rena and her husband, but it was getting too late in the day. I called Rena and told her I would be there the following day to question them.

When I informed Rena of my plans, she said, "I will not be home until six tomorrow evening. My husband is taking a vacation day to stay home and talk to you. Do you have to tell him about my affair with Jim Jamison?"

I said, "If your affair has anything to do with this case, your husband will have to know."

Rena said, "Okay that works for me."

I arrived at the station and went to Tim's desk. He was eating a Big Mac. Tim was always eating something. The way that guy ate he should have weighed around 300 pounds, but he probably only weighed 150. I don't think Tim burned too many calories off from working as I've never seen him do too much of it. I asked Tim if he had any additional information about the library's employees.

Tim said, "It appears our boy Jim Jamison is quite the ladies man. According to two of Mrs. Renton's employees, they had affairs with him. One woman, Celine Selsnick, told me that she recommended Jim Jamison for the maintenance job at the library."

Mrs. Selsnick said, "Immediately after Jim Jamison was hired, he dumped me and started shacking up with Rena. He took her to the same apartment he took me to."

Tim continued, "I checked out Celine Selsnick's alibi. She was in Atlantic City for a weekend junket. She didn't arrive home until Sunday afternoon. Another woman, Pam Oliver, admitted to having a very short affair with

Jim Jamison. It only lasted one night. She also has a solid alibi. I'd like to point out that both of these women are married. It doesn't seem like Jim Jamison fools around with any woman unless they are married." Tim added, "I also called the Ponzett's. Mrs. Ponzetti has agreed to let you question her son Patrick, but only for a few minutes. Mrs. Ponzetti is very protective of her son, or should I say overly protective. I couldn't find anything on Julie Jamison except a few parking tickets. Her boyfriend, Buster, on the other hand, is a different story. I found out the library was broken into about six months ago, and guess who was charged with the break-in? It was Buster Young, Julie's boyfriend."

I told Tim that Julie Jamison mentioned to me that Buster was arrested for a crime, but that he was never charged. I told Tim that however, Julie didn't tell me that Buster was arrested for breaking into the *library*. I called Julie Jamison and asked her why she didn't tell me that Buster was arrested for breaking into the library.

She replied, "Buster was arrested for the break-in, but he was never charged. Actually, he was charged, but the charges were dropped from a lack of evidence. Buster's fingerprints were found in the library, but he told the police that he was there looking for a special book. I told the police that Buster was with me the entire evening the night of the break-in."

"I betcha' that moron Buster doesn't even know how to read," I thought to myself.

Julie continued, "Buster is coming back to Claysville tomorrow for Jamie's funeral. He has agreed to talk to you after we come back from the cemetery. Buster told me he would call and set up a meeting at the police station. Buster didn't think it would be appropriate to talk about Jamie's death in front of my father the day of the funeral."

I thought to myself again, "Boy that Buster sure is a considerate guy. Not!"

I told Tim it sounded like he really had a busy day, and that I would see him in the morning. The poor guy was probably exhausted from questioning two women and making one phone call. I figured that he would probably not have enough energy to make love to his wife. I don't know what Tim's wife sees in him anyway. Well, they say, "There's a match in this world for everyone." Their match seemed like it was made in Purgatory.

Chapter X

Wednesday. They call it: "Over the hump day." God, I hope so. I met Tim at the station, and the two of us drove to the Ponzetti's home. It was around ten in the morning and I noticed that the library was re-opened. I surmised that the forensic team had gathered everything they needed from the crime scene.

I knocked on the Ponzetti's door and Mr. and Mrs. Ponzetti were both there when it opened. I introduced myself. There was no need to introduce Tim, because the Ponzetti's had already met him. I thanked Mrs. Ponzetti for letting me question Patrick.

Mrs. Ponzetti said, "You can question Patrick, but my husband and I want to be present when you do."

Patrick Ponzetti was a big boy, well over 200 pounds. I introduced myself and said, "Hello Patrick, my name is Pete Patrone. I am a detective with the Claysville Police Department and I'd like to ask you a few questions about the murder Saturday night."

Patrick had a surprised look on his face and said, "What murder? I didn't know there was a murder. Who was murdered? Who did it?"

At that point I could tell that Patrick was mentally challenged. I decided a simpler approach. I said, "There was a man working at the library next door Saturday night. Some bad person hit him on the head, and he died. Did you see anyone at the library Saturday night, Patrick?" I quickly retracted my statement and changed my question to, "What time did you go to bed Saturday night, Patrick?"

Patrick said "I always go to bed at 10 o'clock, but some noise kept me awake for a long time. It sounded like a big buzzer or something like that. I looked out my window and saw someone shoveling the snow in the back of the library. I wondered who it was, because I always shovel snow for Mrs. Renton. I thought maybe she didn't ask me to shovel because it was dark, and I have to be home by seven every night. Mrs. Renton pays me to shovel."

I asked Patrick whether it was a man or a woman he saw shoveling.

Patrick said, "It was pretty dark outside; the person was wearing a long coat, so I couldn't tell."

I recalled from my files that there was only a quarter moon that night. Also, there was a light at the rear of the library, but the person who shoveled didn't turn it on. It would have been difficult to recognize anyone that night, more or less tell if it was a man or a woman.

I was asking Patrick these questions because Patrick could see the rear of the library from his bedroom window.

I asked Patrick if he heard any other noises besides the loud buzzing sound.

Patrick thought for a second and then replied, "There was a loud bang on the back door that woke me up."

I asked Patrick if he heard the loud bang before he saw someone shoveling, or after he saw someone shoveling. I told Patrick to take his time and think about this since it was very important. I also told him that his answers might help me catch the bad guy.

Patrick thought a little more and replied, "I heard the bang and it woke me up, and then I went back to sleep. Then the shoveling noise woke me up again."

Evidentially Jamie Jamison never heard someone breaking in because the buffer was running. After breaking in, the murderer probably went into the library and murdered Jamie. I couldn't pinpoint how long the murderer was in the library. Patrick had tried, but it was difficult obtaining a specific time out of him. I surmised that after the crime was committed, the murderer opened the rear door and shoveled the snow to remove any foot prints he or she may have made.

Mr. and Mrs. Ponzetti asked me if I was done questioning Patrick. I told them that I was, and I thanked them for letting me question him.

Patrick asked if I was going to go get the bad guy now. I told him I didn't know who did this bad thing yet.

Chapter XI

I was in my car when I received a call from Buster Young. He asked me what time he could come down the station to be questioned. I could have asked Tim to question Buster, but I thought he might screw it up. It was almost noon and Tim was ready to go to lunch anyway. I still had to question Rena's husband Ed. I told Tim to go to lunch and then look over the facts of the case when he returned to the station. I figured that would keep him busy until he got hungry again. I also asked Tim to look over the finger prints picked up at the library and see if any seemed out of place.

Buster arrived at the station about ten minutes later, and I led him to an interrogation room. I immediately read him his rights. Buster said he didn't need an attorney because he didn't do anything. The first thing I asked Buster was, "Did you find a job while you were away? Your girlfriend said that you left Claysville to see about a job."

Buster gave me a puzzled look and said, "Oh yeah, the job didn't pay enough."

"Pete Patrone, call extension 42" I heard on the public address system. I knew that was Tim's extension. I thought to myself, "Don't tell me the lump found something." When I called Tim he asked me to come to his desk.

I told Buster that I'd be back in a minute. When I arrived at Tim's desk he said, "Guess whose finger prints were found all over the library, including the back door?"

I said, "I'm not playing games Tim. Whose prints are you talking about, Buster Young's?"

Tim answered me in a very disappointing tone, "How did you know?"

I answered, "Tim, my boy, that's why I'm a detective sergeant, and you're just a detective. I've had a bad feeling about that guy Buster since I first met him. Some of those prints could be from the first time he broke into the library.

Tim said, "I didn't know Buster broke into the library."

"There's a lot of things you don't know Pete. That still doesn't explain why Buster may have used gloves to commit the murder. Maybe I'll find out now."

I walked back in the interrogation room and looked at Buster. I said, "Well Buster, I have some very bad news for you. Your finger prints were found all over the library, including the back door."

Buster shot back, "I guess you probably know that I was arrested and charged with breaking into the library six months ago. Those prints could have been there from the last time I broke in."

I said, "Wait a minute stupid, are you admitting that you broke into the library six months ago?"

"Yes, if it will get me out of a murder charge."

I told Buster that the police department kept a record of where any finger prints were found for every case that was investigated. I then told him that this time his prints were found on the back door of the library, and they weren't found there six months ago.

Buster said, "Okay, I broke into the library six months ago through the front door. There was nothing in the library worth stealing, so I took off. Last week I overheard Jim Jamison say that the library had purchased twelve laptops for its patrons. After I dropped Julie off around three in the morning, I decided to break in the library through the back door. It was easy since the back door was wide open. When I entered the library I heard this motor sound. I knew it was Jamie Jamison. I overheard him tell his father that he would finish buffing the floors for him at the library on Saturday night. I had planned on going in, sneaking up on

Jamie from behind, and bopping him on the head. When I walked toward the motor sound, I saw Jamie lying on his back in a pool of blood. I immediately took off out the back door. I didn't even stop to steal a laptop."

I asked Buster what he intended to hit Buster with He told me that he had an old blackjack that his Dad gave him years ago. "My Dad said that it probably wouldn't kill someone, but it would knock them unconscious."

I asked Buster, "Are you sure you didn't bring a pointed red brick with you and hit Jamie in the back of the head?"

Buster said, "I saw a piece of red brick on the floor. I didn't kill Jamie. I'm telling you, he was already dead."

I asked Buster if he shoveled the snow on the rear walk after he went out the door.

Buster said, "I did. I know you cops have ways of checking people's foot prints, even in the snow. I wear heavy motorcycle boots, and there was a lot of snow on the ground that night. I wasn't taking any chances, so I shoveled it. I had a shovel in my car that I use to do Julie's sidewalk with."

I asked Buster if he turned Jamie over. He said, "Why would I turn him over. I knew it was him. I told you that that I overheard Jamie tell his father that he would be there Saturday night, and I also told you that he was on his back lying in a pool of blood."

I said "Okay Buster, I'm going to send my partner in to take a formal statement from you. You are going to be charged with the break-in at the library six months ago. For now, you will also be charged with the break-in Saturday night. You could have a murder charge tacked on to the second break-in. I haven't made up my mind if you're guilty or not of that crime. That will ultimately be a job for our district attorney.

I called Tim and told him the outcome of Buster's questioning. I had to get moving. I told Rena that I would be over some time in the afternoon to question her husband, and it was almost three already.

Chapter XII

The Renton home was probably around one hundred years old, but was well kept. It appeared to have been recently painted. The two roofs seemed to be in pretty good shape too. I looked at all of my suspect's property because I was thinking at taking a stab at real estate. I keep a small binder at my home describing the interior and exterior of all my suspect's homes. I figure it is good practice.

Ed Renton was a large man in his mid fifties. He bore a very long scraggly beard. I guess he didn't own a pair of scissors or one of those ten dollar beard trimmers. My first impression of him was that he was weak. I don't know why I thought that, but I did. I thought that Ed was a very lucky man to still be working at The Works.

I told Ed Renton that I needed to question him about the night of the murder. Ed led me to his spacious Living Room for the questioning. The room was decorated nicely, which I'm sure was Rena's doing.

Ed told me that Rena had made banana bread for the two of us to snack on. I hated banana bread, so I declined Ed's offer. I told Ed that it was too bad I hadn't brought my partner Tim along "I think he would've eaten it all." When I told Ed about my dislike for banana bread he said, "That's okay, it's pretty lousy. Rena's a terrible cook."

I told Ed I would like to start the questioning now.

Ed said, "If you're going to tell me about my wife's affair with Jim Jamison, don't bother. I already know about it. I love my wife, and I know she would come to her senses eventually. I don't blame her for the affair, I blame him. Jim Jamison has a reputation for being a ladies man, and I guess she fell for his BS."

Again I received a surprise from one of my suspects before I even started questioning them. I asked Ed how he knew about his wife's affair.

He replied, "A few of the guys from my plant told me that they saw them together more than once, and that they seemed to be really chummy. Also, a woman that works for Rena at the library called me at work and told me that Rena and Jim were having an affair; I think her name was Celine Selsnick. I told that busy-body that it was none of her business, and to never contact me at my place of employment again. I really do feel sorry for that boy that was murdered. If you ask me it looks like the wrong Jamison was killed."

I thought to myself, "Boy, am I an idiot. Maybe the wrong Jamison *was* killed! After all, they did look very much alike, and they wore the same work uniforms. Maybe someone thought they were striking Jim on the head when it was actually Jamie that they struck." I decided to think along those lines as the investigation progressed.

I asked Ed where he was between the hours of midnight and six in the morning.

"I was attending a union meeting in Detroit. The meeting started at six o'clock Saturday night and it was over at eight. After the meeting, two co-workers and I went to Max's Lounge for a sandwich and drinks. Max's is a lounge located a few blocks from the library."

I told Ed that I was familiar with Max's and then I asked him how long he stayed there.

Ed replied, "I got pretty wasted at Max's and I don't remember the exact time I left. My buddy, Joe Eckles, had to drive me home. My other buddy, Stu Graves, followed us in my car and took Joe back to Max's to pick up his car. I was too drunk to drive. I guess maybe I arrived home around one in the morning, I really don't know."

I asked Ed if Rena was home when he arrived.

He replied, "I don't know. I crashed on the couch. Maybe she'd gone to bed by then."

"Are you sure she wasn't in the chair watching TV?"

He answered, "She might have been. I really don't remember. Don't forget that I was pretty drunk."

I told Ed that I needed the phone numbers of his two buddies to verify his alibi. Just then the two Renton girls entered the room. Ed introduced them as Rita and Ruby. I said to Ed, "With all the R's in this family, I'm surprised your name isn't Ralph or Raul."

Ed said, "You know, that's funny. My real first name is Robert, but I answer to Ed. Edward is my middle name. So I guess all our names start with an R."

Jim's girls told him that they were going to the local mall. Ruby was the sixteen year old girl, and she just recently obtained her driver's license. I'll tell you one thing, they both inherited their Mother's looks. They were on their way to becoming knockouts.

I thanked Ed for his cooperation and told him that I may have to speak to him again. I asked Ed if I could take some banana bread for my partner Tim. "This guy will eat anything," I mused.

Ed said, "I assume you don't like this guy very well."

I said, "He's okay, I guess."

On the way out to my car I noticed some remnants of rose bushes that were in the Renton's front yard. I smiled and thought, "Maybe I should go back and give Ed Mrs. Ponzetti's phone number. She could probably fix Jim up with some nice plastic rose bushes to put in his front yard."

Chapter XIII

I decided to go to the office and call Ed's buddies to verify his alibi. I arrived at the station and went to Tim's desk. He was eating a roast beef sandwich. I took the banana bread out of the bag and threw it on Tim's desk. I said, "Here's some dessert for you. It's banana bread that Rena Renton made for her husband Ed. It's delicious." I filled Tim in as to where I was on the case. I told Tim I was going to call and check Ed Renton's alibi. I figured that both of Ed's buddies would be home because they worked the same shift as Ed. I called Joe Eckels first because he was the one who drove Ed's car home on Saturday night. I asked Joe to tell me exactly what happened on Saturday night at Max's.

Joe said, "Ed Renton, Stu Graves, and I arrived at Max's after a union meeting in Detroit. We all had a sandwich and some drinks. We also watched an old boxing match on TV. At about eleven or so, Ed asked me if I could drive his car home for him. He said he was too drunk to drive. I asked Ed if he was kidding me. My buddy Stu and I probably had about six or seven drinks, but Ed probably only had two or three. Ed kept insisting that I drive his car home for him. I guess he assumed that he was a little too messed up to drive. I know for a fact that Ed had a DUI charge against him a few months ago, and I guess he didn't want to take any chances. I drove Ed in his car to his home. We arrived at his home around 11:eleven-thirty. Stu followed us and I put Ed's car in his garage. Ed thanked me and Stu, and then Stu drove me back to Max's to get my car."

I asked Joe if he saw Rena when he took Ed home Saturday night.

Joe said, "No, I didn't see her at all. You know, come to think of it, her car wasn't in the garage or the driveway either. She must have been out."

I called Ed's buddy Stu and received just about the same story that Joe had given me. I ran a few things through my mind, "Why did Ed lie to me? Where was Rena? Did Buster knock off Jamie? Was Jamie killed by mistake? Why was the body on its back? Why can't I ever get an easy case?" I decided to go back and question Ed Renton again.

When Ed Renton answered his door he asked me why I was at his home again. "Ed, there seems to be a few discrepancies in what you told me about Saturday night. I talked to your friends, and they both said that they didn't think you were too inebriated to drive home Saturday night. They also said that it was eleven-thirty and not one in the morning when they dropped you off. And, they said that your wife was not home Saturday night when they arrived at your house." I continued, "I will have to question Rena again as to where she might have been Saturday night. You can't use your wife for your alibi if she wasn't home. Now, did you go anywhere after your buddies dropped you off Saturday night?"

Ed replied, "I didn't tell you everything that woman Celine told me when she called me at work."

I asked Ed if he was talking about Celine Selsnick.

"Yes, the woman that called me at the plant and told me about my wife's affair. She also told me that Jim Jamison took all of his future conquests to an apartment near Max's lounge." When she called me Celine said, "Jim Jamison took me to that apartment quite a few times. It's a little dump, but he wasn't taking me there for tea and crumpets. The apartment is stocked with beer and assorted varieties of alcohol. Jim also stored little green boxes of candy, imported from Denmark, in his refrigerator. Jim would always give me a box of this candy when we left the apartment. I guess it was his way of rewarding me for sexual favors. If I remember right, I heard Pam Oliver never received a box of candy."

Ed said that Celine asked Jim if he'd ever seen little green boxes of candy in his house.

Ed said, "I told her to mind her own business. I didn't tell Celine that I did recall seeing a few green boxes of candy in the kitchen, and I tried some, and the candy was quite good."

Celine also told Ed that when Rena hired Jim Jamison, she was immediately replaced by Rena.

I asked Ed again where he went Saturday night after his buddies dropped him off at his home.

Jim said, "Before I left the house to go to my meeting I asked Rena what she was going to do while I was gone. She told me she was going to watch a few Cary Grant movies. I called my home Saturday night three or four times and never got an answer. I decided to go to Jim Jamison's apartment and see if she was with him. I told my buddies to drive me home to establish an alibi, in case I caught them together. I don't know what I was going to do if I did. The apartment is on the first floor of a four unit building. There were no cars in front or near the apartment, and there were no lights on either. I decided to return to Max's. I got pretty drunk, but I do recall that it was two in the morning when I arrived home. Rena was not home yet. I thought that maybe she and Jimmy boy had found a new place to shack up. I decided to wait up for Rena to confront her about the affair, but I must have passed out on the recliner. I don't know what time she arrived home. On Sunday morning, Rena told me that Jim Jamison had called her inquiring about his son Jamie. She told me that she was going to meet him at the library. If Rena wasn't with Jim Jamison maybe she found a new friend to have sex with. Maybe it was Jamie Jamison now. I had a lot of weird thoughts going through my mind. When I found out that Jamie had been murdered I didn't know what to think then."

I thanked Ed for the additional information, or should I say the right information. I told Ed he wasn't out of the woods yet and I believed he still could have killed Jamie Jamison. I said that Jamie was killed between the hours of midnight and six in the morning and that he would have had enough time to go to the library and kill Jamie. I told him that perhaps he meant to kill Jim Jamison, but killed Jamie by mistake.

Ed said, "I am not a murderer; I did not kill that boy."

I think I believed him.

I received a call in my car from Tim and he told me he had just talked with the forensics department. They told Tim that the fibers found on the red brick were consistent with the fibers on gloves used at Ed Renton's fabricating plant. Tim thanked me for the banana bread and told me that it was delicious. He asked me if I was currently at the Renton home, and if I was, to pick him up some more banana bread. I sighed and told Tim I was in my car and that I would be going to the Renton's tomorrow, but with a warrant this time.

I went to see the District Attorney, Wynona Williams. I gave her a short synopsis of the case and asked her if I had enough evidence to search the Renton home. Wynona said that I did, and that she would see a judge about issuing one. I told Wynona that I wanted to search the Renton home for the work gloves that may have been used in the murder, and I also requested that the Renton's two automobiles be added to the warrant. Wynona told me that I could pick up the warrant in the morning.

Chapter XIV

Well, day four and I still haven't arrested a suspect for this murder. I arrived at the Renton home with four uniformed police officers and handed the search warrant to Ed Renton.

"What's this?" he asked.

I replied, "This is a search warrant issued by Judge Wise authorizing me and my men to search your home and your automobiles. We also have two officers at the library checking out your wife's automobile."

Ed was angry. "What are you hoping to find?" he asked.

"For one thing, the gloves used to handle the piece of brick used to kill Jamie Jamison," I answered. "They are the same type of gloves used at your plant."

"All those gloves are the same. What could be found in my gloves that you wouldn't find in someone else's?"

I didn't tell Ed, but the fibers in each pair of gloves have their own distinguishing weave.

I told Ed we may also be looking for a crowbar that may have been used to pry open the rear door of the library, as well.

Ed said, "Well good luck there. I don't own a crowbar."

My men and I didn't find anything incriminating in Ed's home, garage, or automobile. I called the two officers who had searched Rena's automobile and they said they had found nothing either.

On the way out of the Renton home, the dried up rose bushes caught my eye. Beside one dried up bush near the sidewalk were three halves of red brick. I saw gash marks and scrapes on the sidewalk where someone may have tried to break the bricks apart. I told one of the officers to put the brick sections in a large evidence bag and take them to the station.

I thought to myself, "Hey, maybe I caught a break here!" A few hours later, I went to the forensics department to see Jerry Claus. Jerry was the senior member of the team. If there was anything credible about these bricks, Jerry would find it.

Jerry said the first brick section he picked up was an exact match to the section found at the murder scene.

I was ecstatic. Now I just had to prove who killed Jamie, Ed or Rena Renton. I would think that Ed Renton did it. He had a much better motive than Rena. I thought to myself, "Why would Rena want to murder Jamie Jamison?"

I decided to concentrate all of my efforts on Ed and Rena. I'm going to set up a meeting with the two of them, together. I telephoned Rena and told her of my intentions.

Rena told me that she was a little tired of being questioned. She said angrily, "You have invaded Ed's and my lives since this crime was committed. This will be the last time that you will question us. You will leave us alone, or charge one of us with murder."

I thought to myself, "That may very well happen after I question the two of you again." I told Rena that I would be at her home on Saturday morning and to make sure that Ed and she were going to be there.

I called Tim at the station and another detective answered the phone. He told me Tim had just left to get something to eat. "What a surprise," I said. I told the detective to call Tim and tell him to call me ASAP. I couldn't reach Tim on his cell. I guess he found a restaurant in a building basement somewhere there was poor reception.

Tim called me back in a few minutes. He said that he'd found a great place for ribs.

I stopped him in mid-sentence and said, "I'm tired of hearing about your eating adventures Tim. I want you to check all of the evidence we have up to this point. I would also like you to go over all of the interview sessions we've conducted." I told Tim I'd see him in the morning.

Thank God our department has installed a new computer system. All of our interview sessions were transferred to the master computer from our laptops. The master computer also has a special file with photos and descriptions of all evidence collected in this case. Tim and I can look back on any aspect of the investigation. Of course, at first, Tim had a hard time with his laptop, but once he got the hang of it he was all right. It took Tim about a week to master logging in without his laptop shutting down.

I decided to get myself something to eat. I didn't tell Tim. I talked to him enough during the day and I sure as hell didn't want to talk to him while I was eating. I decided to go to Max's Lounge. I chose to eat at Max's because almost every aspect of this investigation contains something about that restaurant. It was almost five when I arrived at Max's. I was hoping to make this a working dinner. I assumed that some of the waitresses working now were working the night of the murder. I introduced myself to my waitress, Janet. She was a pleasant woman. She suggested that I order "Max's Cholesterol Special."

I told her that I'd tried one of those before and asked her to suggest something else.

Janet suggested a reuben sandwich. She said that was another of Max's specials.

I told her I'd give it a shot. When the sandwich arrived I couldn't believe my eyes. That sucker was humongous. I wondered if the kitchen made the sandwich a little larger because I was a detective. I knew one thing: I would have half of this thing leftover for my father's dinner. I also knew another thing: I was going to take another extra Lipitor when I took my pills tonight.

Janet stopped at my table and asked me how I liked the sandwich.

I told her that it was the biggest sandwich I had ever eaten, and that it was really good.

Janet told me that "Max's Rueben Special" was a favorite with the Claysville Police Department.

She added, "There's one detective from your department who can eat two of Max's Rueben sandwiches. I think his name is…"

"Tim," I chimed in.

Janet said, "Yea, I guess you would know him. He's a big eater."

I said, "You have no idea."

When Janet brought my check I asked her if she was working the night of the murder and she told me that she was. I asked her if she knew Ed or Rena Renton.

She replied, "I know Ed Renton and a few of his friends from coming in here. He and his friends come in here once a month on Saturday nights after their union meeting in Chicago."

I asked Janet if she was working the past Saturday when Ed Renton came in with his friends.

She replied, "Yes, he was here with two of his friends from "The Works." I think the three of them were here for about three hours and they left around eleven or eleven-thirty."

I asked Janet if Ed Renton may have had a little too much to drink.

She said, "Quite the opposite. Every time I asked Ed if he wanted another drink, he told me no. I wondered why he wasn't drinking that much. I thought he may have not been feeling well. It seemed as if he was preoccupied really. It was unusually slow for a Saturday night. That's why I remember these details so well."

I asked Janet if she knew Rena Renton.

She said that she did and added, "I know her
from the library. I've been there a few times with my son,
and she's the head librarian there. She is very helpful to
everyone, especially the children."

I asked her if she ever saw Rena at Max's Lounge.

"Unfortunately, I have," she said.

I asked her what she meant by "Unfortunately."

Janet looked around the Dining Room and then said,
"I've seen her in Max's four or five evenings with a man
that is not her husband, Ed. At first I thought she was with
a business associate, but I don't think you hold hands with
your business associate, or rub his leg under the table."

I thanked Janet for her cooperation and told her that I
liked the sandwich and that I would be back.

She said, "Bring that Tim guy with you."

I said, "Sure." Speaking of Tim, I decided to give him
a call and see if he found out anything new.

When Tim answered his phone, he told me he may
have something for me, but he wasn't sure. I told Tim to go
ahead, "What are you waiting for?"

Tim said, "I was looking over the results of the search
warrant for Rena Renton's automobile. They found a jack
handle in her trunk with red paint on it. I had forensics
check that paint with the paint on the back door of the
library. And guess what. It's the same paint. But after I
thought about it, I wondered why Rena would pry open
the back door to her library. Didn't she have a key?"

Here I go thinking to myself again. I thought, "I don't
believe it. It seems as if Tim may have found something!"

I told Tim it looked like Rena must have pried the
back door open. I added, "It seems like she wanted us to
think that someone broke into the library, but why?" I told
Tim he did a great job, and that he was to meet me at the
Renton's on Saturday morning.

I still couldn't believe that Tim had found something

beneficial to the outcome of this case. I remembered that I asked Tim to get in contact with Bruce Banter, supposedly Jamie Jamison's only friend. I called Tim back and told him to forget that. I figured that I had enough on Rena to have her charged with first degree murder. I stopped to see the DA to pick up an arrest warrant issued for Rena, based on the information I supplied to her. I called my father and told him I forgot to take something out of the freezer for our evening dinner. I asked him if he had any suggestions and that I would stop on the way home and get some take-out.

"I'm dying to eat some pizza," he chimed in.

"Okay, pizza it is. But you better take your stomach pill right now. The poor guy, on top of dementia and a prostate problem, he had acid reflux. The pills the doctors prescribed for him work pretty well, though. My father worked at Ross Real Estate for forty years before he was forced to retire. They have provided him with an excellent medical program that subsidizes his Medicare. He only pays a fraction of his prescription costs for his medicine. If I worked at a normal job Friday would be my last day of work for the week. I had to wait until the DA had my arrest warrant ready for Rena Renton. Tim had called off sick for the day. I guess he got sick from eating too many of those ribs. I think I'll look over everything that we have so far in this case.

I'm proud of myself. I had suspected Rena Renton from the start of this investigation. That's why they call me "Super Cop." I didn't find anything new in my case files. I was basically wasting time until the DA called me and told me my arrest warrant was ready. When she did call me, it was too late in the day to go to the Renton's. It was almost four in the afternoon and was a good day to leave early. I knew Rena wasn't going anywhere.

I called my Father and asked him if he would like a

fish sandwich instead of pizza for dinner. I reminded him that I told him to take a pill for his stomach and he said that he forgot to take it. He told me I must have read his mind and that he would love to have a fish sandwich. There was a church right down the street from our house that served fish sandwiches every Friday. They used to serve fish and assorted sides during Lent only, but it was such a money maker they decided to offer the food every Friday year-round. Tables and chairs and a take-out booth are located in the social hall next to the church area. I picked up two sandwiches, fries, and coleslaw. I don't attend church regularly, but I stopped in to and thank God for letting my father win a bingo game.

Tim and I arrived at the Renton's Saturday morning. Rena answered the door. I told her that I would like to speak to her first, and then to her husband.

Rena said that I could speak to her and Ed together. She told me that it was okay if her husband was present during our questioning. She led us into the living room where Ed was sitting in his recliner.

Ed Renton didn't seem too happy, but he said hello to us anyway.

I apologized to the Renton's for inconveniencing them again. I told them that from our investigation that Tim and I thought that they were both suspects in the murder of Jamie Jamison. I continued, "Our investigation has leaned toward you Rena. I really would like to speak to you in private."

Ed Renton said, "I'm staying here. I'd like to hear what you have to say to my wife."

I was a little shocked at Ed's attitude. Maybe he wasn't a wimp after all. I told Ed that he could stay in the room while I spoke to Rena. I looked at Rena and said, "It appears to my partner Tim and me that you killed Jamie Jamison. We think you went out the back door of the library, locked the door, and then pried it open to make it look as if it was a robbery attempt. We also think that you pried open the drawers in your desk to bolster the robbery attempt scenario. You performed these two actions after you snuck up on Jamie Jamison, who you thought was Jim Jamison, and struck him in the back of his head with a red brick. Your motive was that you were trying to silence Jim Jamison because of your love affair with him. Jim Jamison told me about his threat to tell your husband about the affair. It's a shame that you and Ed couldn't be truthful with each other. If you had been, I don't think this murder would have been committed. We have the murder weapon, the section of red brick. We have your jack handle you used to pry open the back door of the library. We also have the fibers from the gloves used to handle the red brick. We didn't find the gloves, so we assumed that you disposed of them after the murder. Mrs. Rena Renton, I have an arrest warrant here for the first degree murder of Jamie Jamison. My partner Tim will now read you your rights." Rena seemed shocked. After Tim read Rena her rights, he told her that she would have to go to the station with us.

I told Ed Renton that there would be nothing he could do at the station and that he might as well stay home. I informed Rena that we were going to take her to the station where she would be formally charged. I also informed her that she would spend the night as a guest of the Claysville Police Department.

Sometime during my conversation with the Renton's, Tim disappeared. I couldn't believe it. I found him in the kitchen finishing the banana bread.

Chapter XV

Rena was formally arraigned when Pete and I arrived at the station. In a perfect world I would ask Rena for a confession and she would say, "Okay." I thought, what the hell, I'll take a shot. I said, "Mrs. Renton, we have enough evidence to convict you of first degree murder of Jamie Jamison. It would be to your advantage if you gave me a full confession."

Rena said that she had thought about it and decided that she wanted to give me her confession. She told me that her life was a wreck and that she didn't want her life on display in a public trial. She said, "I'd like to protect my husband and my daughters from any embarrassment."

I couldn't believe what I was hearing. I was going to get my confession. I told Rena again that she was entitled to an attorney.

"Thanks Pete, I don't need an attorney," she said.

I set up my tape recorder and told Rena to give me her confession starting with Saturday night when she entered the library.

Rena's first line was, "I killed Jamie Jamison, but it was a mistake." Rena continued, "My love affair with Jamie's father was the main reason for Jamie's death. I had an ongoing affair with Jamie's Father, Jim Jamison, for the past three months. On Friday, December 5th, I had a conversation with Jim Jamison. He told me that he was falling in love with me. I told him that I didn't love him, and that I was in our affair for the sex only. I also told him that I thought that we should end our affair immediately. Jim told me that he would give me until Sunday, December 7th, to rethink our situation. He said that if our affair wasn't continued he would call my husband and tell him about us. I love my husband, and I didn't want him to find out about my affair. That's when I decided to kill Jim."

"I knew Jim Jamison was going to be working Saturday night, going into Sunday morning, buffing the floors of my library. I decided if I was going to do this that I needed a weapon. I didn't own a gun, and I wouldn't know how to use one anyway. I've read quite a few murder mysteries at my library. I recalled one murder mystery where the murder weapon was a section of brick with a protruding piece of concrete on it. I decided that was going to be my weapon. I perused several websites on the Internet showing vulnerable locations on the rear of the human head. From these sites I knew the various locations on the head that would, if hit with brute force, cause death. I recalled seeing some old red bricks in my front yard. I went out that evening and broke a brick apart on my sidewalk. Things were working out. The brick had a large protruding point on it similar to the one I read about in the murder mystery."

"I went to the library at around one-thirty on Sunday morning, the 7th of December. I parked my car a block away from the rear entrance of the library. I went to the rear entrance and laid my jack handle on the stoop because I would need it later to pry open the rear door. I entered the front door of the library and heard the sound of the buffing machine. I took this noise as an advantage for me because it would let me sneak up on Jim and whack him in the back of his head. I really didn't know what I would have done if he had turned around when I was sneaking up on him. Besides being a great lover, Jim was a great worker. He was very meticulous about any job he performed. Now I know his son Jamie was as well. I saw who I thought was Jim in the murder mystery aisle. At the time I thought that was quite ironic: a murder committed in the murder mystery aisle."

"I snuck up on him from behind, and I lifted the piece of brick high into the air. I made sure that the protrusion would be the first thing to hit Jim's head. Bam! I drove that hunk of brick into Jim's skull as hard as I could. A huge mass of blood squirted from his head and he began to fall back. I gave Jim a shove so he would fall forward. Although I had worn some throw-away clothes, I didn't want to get any more blood on them than I had too.

"I decided to turn Jim over and make sure that he was dead. Jim weighed over 200 pounds but I managed to turn him over. That's when I discovered it was Jamie I struck on the head, and not Jim. I checked Jamie's pulse and there was none. He was dead. I felt bad about killing that innocent kid. I didn't know what to do then. I had to get my head together.

"I decided to carry out my plan as I had rehearsed it in my mind the night before. I opened the back door of the library and retrieved my jack handle. I turned the light on for the rear of the library. That was a mistake. That's when I saw Patrick, the boy next door, looking out of his bedroom window. I didn't know what else to do, so I waved at him. I went back into the library to my desk and pried open a few of the drawers. I wanted to make it look like it was a robbery attempt gone wrong. There were a lot of homeless people and transients who milled around the library at all hours. I was hoping that the police would think one of them broke into the library.

"I went to the back of the library, turned the light on, and opened the back door. I looked towards Patrick's window and saw him looking at me. I waved at him again. I went out on the stoop and shut and locked the back door. I used my jack handle to pry open the rear door. I went back in the library to make sure I didn't forget to do anything. I remembered seeing the bloody red brick on the floor near Jamie's body. I decided to leave it there, since I was wearing

Ed's gloves when handling it. I figured that usually most murderers are stupid people. If they killed someone, they would panic and forget to retrieve the murder weapon. I left mine at the front door.

"On my way home, I stopped at the rear alley of a Chinese restaurant. There was a huge dumpster there. I remembered to take a filled gas can with me when I left my house. Thank God the dumpster was empty. The refuse company must have emptied it already. I put the bloody gloves and clothes in the dumpster and poured a little gasoline on them. I didn't want a huge fire that would draw attention; I just wanted to make sure the items burned. When I arrived home Ed was passed out on his recliner. I went to bed, but I had trouble sleeping. The last thing I remember was wondering why Jamie was at the library and not Jim."

I had Rena write and sign a confession as a back-up for the verbal one. It wasn't exactly what I was looking for, but it would do. I called one of the secretaries in and gave her the recorded confession to be transcribed. I asked Rena if she had anything to add that wouldn't be part of her confession. I was curious myself why Jamie Jamison was at the library and not Jim Jamison.

Rena continued, "It was early Sunday morning when I committed the murder. I intended to go to work Monday morning and call 911 to state that I discovered Jamie's body. Well, it didn't work out that way. Jim Jamison called my home Sunday morning. I thought he was calling to tell my husband about our affair. I told him I wouldn't let him talk to my husband. Jim told me that he didn't call to talk to Ed. He told me that he thought about me all day Saturday and decided I just wasn't worth it. Jim told me that Jamie had worked for him Saturday night. He wanted to meet me at the library to see if Jamie might have had an accident. Drama was my secondary in college. I finally had an opportunity to use it on Sunday morning. I had to act shocked when we discovered Jamie's body. I even managed to shed a few tears.

"I remember thinking if Jim would have called me sooner and told me he wasn't going to tell my husband about our affair, I wouldn't have planned to murder him, and his son would be alive today. I asked Jim again why he wasn't working at the library Saturday night. He told me that he asked Jamie to work for him because he wasn't feeling well. He told me that he was so upset about me that he asked Jamie to finish the floors for him. I truthfully think that Jim Jamison should share in the guilt for his son's murder."

I told Rena that it didn't work that way. I also told her that although she thought she was killing Jim Jamison, it didn't matter that she killed Jamie Jamison. "You still committed a murder," I told her.

I peered into Rena's eyes and said, "You know Rena, I really like you. I find it hard to believe that you could commit such a cold blooded murder."

Rena told me that Robert Louis Stevenson wrote a fantastic book, "Dr. Jekyll and Mr. Hyde." She went on, "It details a man's life of good and evil and his living with two separate personalities. I imagine the Dr. Jekyll side of me is the happy wife and librarian. I imagine the Hyde side of me is the unfaithful wife and cold blooded killer."

Rena asked if we were done. "I'm exhausted," she informed me.

I told her I was going to see that she got to her cell so she could get some rest and that she would spend a few days and nights in our jail until a bail hearing was scheduled for her. Before they took Rena away, I told her that she should seriously think about contacting an attorney. I asked her if she wanted to call her husband.

She answered, "No, I'm sure he'll be in tomorrow."

I felt guilty that I was acting so concerned. I knew the reason. I know I talked Rena into that confession.

Chapter XVI

The following day Ed Renton came to the station to visit his wife and she told him she was advised to seek out an attorney. Rena asked Ed how her daughters were. Ed said that he told the girls that there was a huge mistake and that their Mother would be home in a few days. Ed added, "I think they're more concerned about their image in school than they are about having their Mother arrested for murder."

Ed told Rena that he had made arrangements with an attorney and her name was Sarah Stein. "She is an excellent defense attorney and she will be in to visit you this afternoon, he said."

Ed then looked at Rena lovingly and said, "Rena, did you kill Jamie Jamison?"

Rena looked at Ed shamefully and said, "Honey, I'm afraid that I did. I did it for us. Jim Jamison was going to reveal my affair with him, and I thought if you found out, you would leave me. I didn't want to lose you; I love you so very much."

Ed was still in a state of shock, even though he did suspect Rena had killed Jamie. He said, "I wish you would have said something to me first and then we could have somehow worked this out. I love you very much as well and I would do anything to keep you in my life. I'm afraid to say that I knew about your affair for over two months now. I was waiting for you to come to your senses. If only you would have confided in me, this whole mess would never have happened."

Ed kissed Rena good-bye and told her he would return the following day. As Ed was leaving the cell he said,

"Call me this evening after you've spoken to the attorney. I've taken the rest of the week off from the plant. I'm taking pizza home for the girls and me to have for dinner tonight."

Chapter XVII

Sarah Stein arrived at the station a few hours later and was admitted to Rena's cell. She introduced herself to Rena and said, "I have been retained by your husband to represent you in the murder of Jamie Jamison."

Rena looked at Sarah and thought, "She has the ugliest hair style I've ever seen on a woman. I hope she takes better care of her clients than she takes care of her hair."

Sarah's hair was three shades of red, cut into four or five different lengths, and looked like it needed washed. She was a petite woman and probably didn't weight one-hundred pounds. Sarah wore an expensive diamond necklace and bracelet set. She was wearing a black business suit with a man's white mock tie and Rena noticed that she wasn't wearing a wedding ring. Rena thought it would be a little precocious of her to ask Sarah if she was married, so she didn't.

Sarah opened her briefcase and pulled out a copy of Rena's confession. "Big mistake, big mistake,"

Sarah said. "Were you advised of your rights by the arresting detective?"

Rena replied, "Yes, I was."

Then Sarah said, "Why then did you give him this confession? You should have asked for an attorney at that very moment."

Rena said, "The detective was Pete Patrone and I told him I didn't need an attorney."

Sarah sarcastically said, "Oh, the so called Super Cop. Say no more! I'm going to see if I can get this confession thrown out and omitted from your file. I don't trust Pete Patrone at all. I've found out from the District Attorney that a bail hearing will be held for you on Monday morning at ten. That will give me the weekend to see what I can dig up by then. Don't worry Rena, I'll be ready for them."

By law, the defense attorney has the right to all of the same information as the DA concerning the suspect. Sarah obtained all of this information from the District Attorney, Wynona Williams. Wynona Williams has been the Claysville District Attorney for three years. She has an excellent reputation as a prosecuting attorney, similar to Sarah's reputation as a defense attorney. Neither of these two women had lost case so far.

That night, Sarah poured herself a small glass of chardonnay. She laid out all the documents pertaining to the case on a huge table in her den. "It's going to be a long night," she said to herself.

She woke up at that table at three in the morning and arose to go to bed. She had a morning cup of coffee and started right back where she left off. She looked at everything on her table and thought, "There's got to be something here; there usually is." Sarah was looking at the search warrant for the Renton home when her face brightened up. She said out loud, "I'm going to get that confession thrown out. In fact, I'm going to get the whole murder charge dropped."

Rena was taken from her cell to the courtroom for the ten o'clock bail hearing. Her pale green prison garb was a far cry from the casual business suits she wore at the library. Sarah was sitting at a table waiting for Rena. Sarah noticed that Rena seemed to be a little depressed, and rightfully so. Sarah told Rena that she had nothing to worry about. Rena looked at Sarah a little puzzled. After all, she had confessed to a murder.

In attendance at the hearing were Ed Renton, Jim Jamison and his daughter Julie, and Detective Pete Patrone. There was no sign of Buster. I think courtrooms probably scared him. I found out from Ed Renton that his daughters went to Rena's sister's home for the weekend.

Judge Pete Wise entered the courtroom and the bailiff called the court to order. Judge Wise was known to be a fair man and he was also known to be a stickler for detail. The Judge asked the bailiff to tell him what the first case scheduled for the day was.

The Bailiff said, "The State of Illinois verses Mrs. Rena Renton, your honor."

Judge Wise asked the District Attorney to read the charges against Mrs. Renton.

"Mrs. Renton has been charged with the first degree murder of Jamie Jamison," Wynona stated. "Mrs. Renton has confessed to the murder of Jamie Jamison and although Mrs. Renton is a librarian for The Claysville Library the State thinks she is a threat to our society. In her confession Mrs. Renton admitted to the brutal and premeditated murder of said victim. Although Mrs. Renton claims that she killed the wrong man, the intent was still there. Because this is a murder charge, the State is asking for a bail of $500,000."

Judge Wise asked Sarah Stein if she had anything to say in defense of her client.

Sarah said, "I do. I would like your honor and the State of Illinois to dismiss the first degree murder charge against my client."

Judge Wise said, "On what grounds?"

"On the grounds of an illegal search," Sarah said.

Sarah walked up and handed a copy of the search warrant to Judge Wise. On the way back to her desk she handed a copy to the DA, Wynona Williams. Sarah continued, "I'd like your honor and the District Attorney to look at the center of the page hi-lighted, "Area of Search." It clearly specifies the areas of the search should be my client's automobile, her husband's automobile, the attached garage, and the interior of the house on 420 Dunster Street. The prosecutions main article of evidence against my client is the murder weapon: the piece of bloody red brick. The other half of that red brick was discovered on my client's front yard, clearly the exterior of my client's home. This warrant states nothing about searching the exterior of my client's home on 420 Dunster Street. Therefore this warrant is null and void, and all charges should be dropped against my client."

Judge Wise told the District Attorney that Miss Stein had an excellent argument. The judge asked Miss Williams why he should see any reason why the charges should not be dropped against Mrs. Renton.

Wynona was still in a state of shock. She gave a nasty look towards Pete Patrone, and then addressed Judge Wise. Wynona replied, "No, Your Honor, I can see no reason why the murder charge can not be dropped against Mrs. Renton. I would, although, like to keep my option open to re-file the murder charge against Mrs. Renton at a later date when other evidence will be produced."

Judge Wise informed Wynona that her option to re-file was dully noted.

Ed Renton ran up to Rena and gave her a big hug. He shook Sarah's hand and thanked her. Sarah told Ed and Rena that they weren't out of the woods yet. She said, "The DA must find more evidence. She can no longer use the bloody brick. She may try to find a witness, or she may re-introduce Rena's jack handle as evidence."

Rena and Ed left the courtroom.

The District Attorney caught up to me as I was leaving the courtroom. She said rather nastily "How could you let this happen, Pete?"

I said, "I know I missed the word 'exterior' on the search warrant, but it was your office that typed the warrant. I think we should both should share the blame on this one.

Don't worry though. We both know that this woman is guilty. I will find something else on her, and you can re-file your charges."

Wynona said, "You better!"

Chapter XVIII

After leaving the courtroom, I went straight to Tim's desk. I told him about the murder charge being dismissed against Rena.

He looked at me and said, "What the hell are you going to do now?"

I replied, "We're going to find more evidence against this woman. There has to be something that we missed. Everyone knows now that she killed that kid. Maybe someone will come forwards."

Tim told me he'd get right back on the case after he returned from an early lunch. I could see where his priorities were.

I sat at my desk wondering what my next move should be. I decided I was going to question Patrick Ponzetti again. Patrick's parents had only let me speak to him for five minutes. Things would be different this time. I left a note on Tim's desk and told him to interview all of Rena's co-workers again because we needed more evidence to re-charge her for the murder.

I called Tim while I was driving to the Ponzetti residence. He answered and told me that he read my note.

I said, "Tim, listen to me. I forgot one very important thing. Tell Rena's co-workers to say nothing about you telling them she murdered Jamie Jamison. Do you understand that?"

Tim answered in his usual clueless way, "Uh, I guess."

I arrived at the Ponzetti's and Mrs. Ponzetti answered the door. She said rather angrily, "What do you want now? I think we answered all of your questions."

I told Mrs. Ponzetti that Rena had confessed to Jamie's murder but that she was released on a technicality. I told her that I needed to re-question the three of them, but especially Patrick. I assured her that I would be as gentle as I could with him, and that she could be present for the questioning.

I had a copy of the first questions and answers given to me by the Ponzettis'. In this questioning period they said pretty much the same as the first period. I asked them to call Patrick into the room. I was ready to ask Patrick some more detailed questions.

I asked Patrick how he was doing today.   He told me that he was tired because he'd been doing a lot of work at the library. I asked Mrs. Ponzetti if Patrick was working more at the library than he usually did.

She replied, "Ever since that murder, Patrick has been there working every day. He normally works at the library a couple days a week."

I returned my attention to Patrick and asked, "Do you like Rena Renton, Patrick?"

"Her name is Mrs. Renton and I like her a lot. She always gives me money for doing jobs at the library."

I asked Patrick again if he saw or heard anything last Saturday night. I reminded Patrick about what he said the last time we talked. You said, "I saw someone shoveling the walk near the back door, and you said that you heard a loud buzzing sound."

Patrick looked at me, and then he looked at his parents. He said, "I saw something else, but I'm not allowed to tell you. I told my Mom and Dad, but they said that I couldn't tell anyone else."

I told Mr. and Mrs. Ponzetti they could get themselves in a lot of trouble by holding information from me.

They told Patrick that he could tell me what else he saw that night. I assured Patrick that he wouldn't get in trouble for telling me what else he saw. Patrick said, "I saw a light go on in the back of the library. I looked toward the light and saw Mrs. Renton. She looked up and saw me looking at her, and then she waved at me. Then I got real confused. Mrs. Renton put a big bar in the back door and broke it."

I asked Patrick if it could have been a screwdriver or a jack handle.

"I don't know, but it was real long," Patrick replied.

I then asked Patrick, "Are you sure that Mrs. Renton came out of the back door, closed it, and then put the big knife in it?"

Patrick replied, "Yes, she came out of the back door, and then she closed it. Then she turned around and put the big knife in it. I wondered why she didn't use her key to open the door; she's the boss over there, you know."

I asked Patrick if Mrs. Renton ever talked to him about what happened that night.

Patrick replied, "Yes, on Monday she told me not to tell anyone that I saw her at the back door. She gave me a twenty dollar bill, and told me that it was our little secret. When I got home I gave the twenty dollar bill to my dad to hold for me. I've never had a twenty dollar bill before. My dad asked me where I got it. I told him I wasn't allowed to tell anybody where I got it, but that I got it for not saying what I saw. My dad told me I could tell him, but nobody else. Mrs. Renton is going to be mad at me because I told on her."

I almost forgot to ask Patrick the most important question of all. "What time did you see Mrs. Renton?"

Patrick said that he had a big clock on his bedroom wall that glows in the dark. He said that his Mom gave it to him for his fifteenth birthday. "I looked at my glowy clock when I saw Mrs. Renton and it said one o'clock."

I told the Ponzettis' that I didn't think Patrick should

work at the library for a while because I had a feeling that Rena Renton was going to be replaced. I called Wynona from my car and told her I had a witness in the Jamison murder. I gave her the details, and then asked if she had enough to re-file charges against Rena.

Wynona said, "The first thing you should do is get permission from the boy's parents so he can testify." Wynona continued, "Didn't you say that the boy was mentally challenged? I will have to speak to him. I want to see how mentally challenged he is and I would also like to see if a jury will accept his testimony as truth. After you receive the parent's permission, bring the boy down here so I can speak to him. We can't use the brick as evidence again but we can use Mrs. Renton's jack handle."

I went back to the Ponzetti house and anticipated both of them giving me a difficult time. I told the Ponzettis' that Patrick would have to tell a jury what he'd seen and that I would need their permission to have Patrick testify.

Mrs. Ponzetti said, "My Patrick likes Mrs. Renton and she likes him. My husband and I think she is a nice woman."

"You may think Mrs. Renton is a nice woman, but she has murdered a boy that's around the same age as your son. We need Patrick to testify. That woman needs to be punished for taking another human beings life."

Mrs. Ponzetti told me she would talk it over with her husband and call me in the morning with her decision.

I called Tim and told him about the new development. Tim said, "What's the difference if the kid saw Rena Renton prying open the back door?"

I angrily answered Tim, "You idiot, if she pried open the back door after she came out of the library, it means that she'd already committed the murder. She pried open the door to make it look as though someone tried to break in. If you recall, when we discovered the red paint on Rena's jack handle she said, "I used the jack handle to pry open the back door because I'd forgotten my key for the front door. This woman is a liar extraordinaire. The Ponzetti kid told me that the light went on, she waved at him, and then she pried open the back door. And the most important thing he told me was that the time he saw Rena Renton was around one o'clock. That puts her in the timeline for the murder. I think this woman's goose is cooked."

After trying to absorb everything I told him, Tim replied with, "Oh."

Chapter XIX

Well it was Tuesday again and time for my father's bingo day at the Senior Center. I wonder if God had another mini miracle in store for me. It would be nice if my father won something again. He was so excited last week. I said a little prayer hoping God would help me out again. My father asked if he could use his gift certificate for Max's for dinner tonight.

I told him that I would leave work a little early so we could go to Max's. I wanted to avoid the dinner crowd, so I told him I would pick him up at four. Boy, I really love that man. I'll really miss him when he's gone. I dropped him off in front of the center, wished him luck, and told him I'd see him at four.

I arrived at my desk a little late because of dropping my father off. I couldn't believe that Tim was at his desk already. Of course, he was eating. In fact, he offered me one of his greasy burrito breakfast sandwiches. I thanked him, but told him I'd eaten already, even though I hadn't. All I ever have in the morning is black coffee. I asked Tim if the Ponzetti's had called yet. Before he could answer me, someone on the public address system said that I had an incoming call.

It was Mrs. Ponzetti and she to me, "Detective Patrone, my husband and I have talked it over, and we've decided to let Patrick testify. We made our decision after you told us that Mrs. Renton killed a boy as old as our Patrick."

I told Mrs. Patrick, "May have killed; not killed a boy as old as Patrick."

Her response was, "Whatever."

Boy, I hate that word.

"I'm going to put my husband on the phone now to get directions to your police station," she added.

I asked Mrs. Ponzetti if she wanted me to send a patrol car to pick up the three of them. I added, "Maybe Patrick would enjoy a ride in a police car."

Mrs. Ponzetti replied, "Heavens no. Don't try to pick us up in one of your police cars. I don't want our neighbors thinking you are taking us to jail."

The Ponzetti family arrived about a half an hour later. Patrick was dressed up in a black suit. I told Mrs. Ponzetti that Patrick really looked nice.

She said, "I thought we were supposed to dress him up nice. The people I see on television in courtrooms are always wearing suits. Patrick only has one suit and we save it for funerals. We really can't afford to buy him another one, so he wore his funeral suit today."

I told Mrs. Ponzetti that she must have misunderstood me again. I said, "We wanted Patrick to talk to the district attorney, Wynona Williams." I added, "A lot of other legal things have to happen until Patrick can testify." I didn't dare tell her that Wynona wanted to find out if a jury would believe Patrick's testimony. I asked Mrs. Ponzetti if I could take Patrick into Wynona's office.

She said, "Can my husband and I go in with Patrick? He talks a lot better when we are with him."

I checked with Wynona and she said, "That will be alright for today Pete. But tell the Ponzettis that when Patrick testifies, he will have to sit on the stand alone."

Patrick told the same story to Wynona that he told me. He told Wynona that his parents told him he was allowed to tell her his and Mrs. Renton's secret. Wynona gave the Ponzettis' a mild scolding about withholding evidence. I thought she was going to blow the whole thing right there, but surprisingly they accepted the light tongue lashing.

Wynona came to me after she questioned Patrick and told me that she was pleased with the way Patrick responded to her questions. She said, "I applied a little bit of pressure on Patrick. I know that Sarah Stein will do the same when she questions him on the stand." Wynona added, "After hearing Patrick speak, the jury would surely know Patrick was mentally challenged and if Sarah applied too much pressure on Patrick, she would not look good in the eyes of the jury."

I thanked the Ponzettis' for coming down, and told them the next time I contacted them was when Patrick was to testify. I was getting ready to leave when Wynona called me into her office. She told me she thought she had enough evidence on Mrs. Renton to re-file the murder charges and that she needed four or five hours to have a new arrest warrant prepared. She said that she may have the warrant ready in time for me to serve Mrs. Renton at the library.

I said, "Why don't we let her get a good night's sleep. She's at the library at nice tomorrow morning. I'll arrest in the morning." I also just remembered I promised my father I would pick him up at four to take him to dinner tonight. I thought there could be no harm in waiting until the morning to serve Rena with the new arrest warrant. How wrong I was.

Chapter XX

Despite the very cold weather, my father was waiting for me on the front porch. I asked him why he didn't wait for me inside the house.

"Cold weather is good for the blood," he said.

I told him I tried a reuben sandwich at Max's and that it was quite delicious. I also told him there was a nice waitress who worked there that would be easy on his eyes.

"You should take her out on a date," he said.

I told him that I wasn't ready to date anyone yet.

He said, "What are you waiting for? You've been divorced for almost two years now. Please don't let me hold you back. If worse comes to worse, when you get married, I'll move into one of those old people homes."

I said, "Hold on Pops, first you want me date, now you want me to marry, and then put you in a home."

"Remember, you just do what you have to do," he said.

I had made the right move going to Max's early since the place was nearly empty. Thank God Janet was working. I wanted my Father to meet her. Maybe I was attracted to her. It has been so long, I can't even tell when I am attracted to someone.

Janet recognized me right away. "Oh, I see you've brought a friend with you to try one of Max's sandwiches."

"Actually, Janet, this is my father Pete, senior," I said.

Janet said, "You're kidding me. He doesn't look old enough to be your father."

My father said, "I like her Pete. Ask her to marry you right now."

Janet seemed a little embarrassed and said, "Are you gentlemen ready to order?"

I ordered two Rueben sandwiches. I asked my father if he was as bad as I was in figuring out a woman's age. I was still worried that Janet was too young for me. "Hell, I didn't even know if she was married or not," I thought to myself.

My father was about to answer me when Janet brought our sandwiches. You know how old people are. It seems to me that after they reach a certain age they think they can say, or ask anyone anything.

To my amazement my Father said to Janet, "My son wants to go out on a date with you, but he's afraid you're too young for him. He's fifty-eight. How old are you?"

If I thought she was embarrassed before, I knew she was embarrassed now.

"I will not tell you my age, but I will tell you I'm not fifty yet," Janet said as she regained her composure. She looked at me and said, "If you were to ask me out, I think I would say yes."

"You'll have to excuse my Father," I said. Now I was embarrassed. Wait until I get him home.

I told Janet that I was wrapping up a case and I would call her when things quieted down a little. She gave me her phone number. I looked over and saw that my father seemed to be done eating. I knew he couldn't finish the whole sandwich. I had Janet wrap the other half and put it in a container. I told my father that he embarrassed me and Janet as well.

He said, "You have to open your mouth today if you want to get anywhere. I fixed you up. You should be thanking me instead of balling me out."

I guess he was right. I gave in and thanked him for being so helpful.

Chapter XXI

I arrived at the library the next morning at nine to serve the arrest warrant on Rena. The front door was locked. I knocked on the door a few times and got no reply. I saw Rena's car parked in its usual space. I tried the door again. Something just didn't feel right to me. I called out Rena's name and there was still no reply. I decided to go around the library to the back door. If I thought a crime had been committed, I didn't need a search warrant to break into the library. I knew that the back door was much smaller and lighter than the front one. When I arrived at the back door, I didn't have to break it down because it was wide open. I entered and shouted out Rena's name. There was no response.

I walked toward Rena's desk and spotted her sitting in her chair. Rena appeared to have been shot. I checked her vital signs and she was dead. I recalled that I was going to arrest Rena the night before, but I'd changed my mind to take my father to dinner. If I wouldn't have, Rena probably would be alive today. I called the station and told them to send down the coroner and the forensics team. I knew that they didn't need directions since they had been here before.

Well, one murder case was almost terminated, but I guess I'll have to start another one. When I first met Rena, I suspected her of Jamie's death. I have that special knack for reading people, and I'd read Rena well. I believe I already know who committed this murder. My initial suspicion was Jim Jamison. I believe he may have murdered Rena in retribution for her murdering his son Jamie. I could be wrong, but I don't think so. I didn't see a murder weapon and I didn't think Rena would commit suicide.

I called Tim and told him about discovering Rena's body. I told him to locate Jim Jamison and tell him I wanted to talk to him. I waited for the coroner to arrive.

Dr. Meenan's team arrived and he gave me his preliminary report. "Well Pete, another murder, huh? I don't see you for six months and now twice in two weeks. I guess December is a popular month for murder. Tell me something Pete, isn't this the woman who discovered the body of the young boy here a couple of weeks ago?"

I said, "Doc, you might not believe this, but this is the woman who killed that young boy. We have definite evidence tying this woman to the boy's murder."

The Doctor said, "You're right Pete. Anyone else might not believe you, but knowing you, I believe you. Oh, by the way, forensics found a .38 spent shell on the floor. It was under that small book stool over there."

The doctor was pointing to the "Murder Mystery aisle."

It appears that the murderer shot Rena, and the shell fell to the floor beneath him. In his haste he must've kicked the shell with his shoe when he left. I thought that maybe the murderer might have looked for the shell, but couldn't find it. Apparently the murderer didn't know that he'd kicked it under the book stool.

I saw Doctor Meenan leaving. On his way out, he told me that he would have a detailed report on Rena later on in the day. I asked him at what time he thought the murder was committed.

He replied, "From the condition of the body I would say only an hour or two at most. It looks like you might have arrived right after the victim was shot."

I found the previous sign that Rena had made when Jamie was murdered. I had to post the sign on the front door telling patrons that the library was closed until further notice, again. I never imagined the same sign would be hanging on the front door because of Rena's murder.

I felt a little sorry for the library's patrons. If murders continued to be committed in the library, it may never re-open.

Some of the library's employees were starting to report for work. I called Tim and told him to get his ass down here and start questioning the employees again. I had my own ideas how the murder may have gone down. I started to make notes to confirm my thoughts with forensics.

As I mentioned previously, the back door was wide open. It didn't appear that anything in the library was moved or taken. The drawers in Rena's desk were repaired. It seemed to me that Rena must have known the murderer. I surmised the murderer may have set up a meeting with Rena and that's why the back door was open. That would explain why there was no sign of a forced entry. I also surmised that the murderer stopped in front of Rena's desk, maybe conversed with her a little, and then shot her in the head. Again, my mind told me that the obvious suspect would be Jim Jamison. I was waiting for Tim to see if he ever got in touch with Jim.

In the meantime, I got a call from Doctor Meenan. He told me he completed the autopsy sooner than he thought and wanted to see me.

I was hoping the Doc had some startling news for me since I sure could use some. When I arrived at his office he said, "There's nothing unusual here. We have a female in her mid forties shot at close range with a .38 caliber handgun. The bullet entered the front of the cranial area and death was instantaneous. That's basically all I have."

I asked him, "Can you give me the murderer's name?"

The Doc answered me with a smile on his face, "Sorry Pete, I did my job. And again, you have to do yours."

Chapter XXII

Tim called me and said that he talked to Jim Jamison. Jim told him that he would be home the entire day and that I could stop over any time. From the way Tim described Jim's attitude, he sounded almost friendly. I wonder what had got into Jamison.

I arrived at Jamison's home and told him that Rena had been murdered.

"Oh my God, no," he said, as a few tears ran smoothly down his face.

I think this bastard murdered Rena or had something to do with it. I also think that, like Rena, he may have studied drama in college. I offered my condolences regarding Rena's death. I figured that after all, they had been close at one time. I asked Jim where he was at the time of the murder, between six and nine this morning.

Jim said, "I just started a new job at a local office building. I was working with two other guys from four to nine in the morning. I will write their names and telephone numbers down for you."

It seemed as though Jim was ready for me. He had two witnesses for his alibi. I called Tim and gave him the names of Jim's co-workers. I told him to check these two men for any prior arrests. Jim Jamison was too sure of himself.

I asked Jim if I could take a look at his hideaway apartment. I told him I could get a search warrant if needed. At the moment, I couldn't get one to search the apartment. I didn't have any evidence to warrant a warrant. I thought I'd take a shot and see if he would agree to a search.

Jim said, "There's nothing there you'd want to see, but if you want to, we can take a drive over there right now."

I thanked him for his cooperation and told him I would follow him in my car. I thought that I might see something incriminating in Jim's apartment. Every aspect of this case contains something involving Jim's bachelor apartment.

While following Jim to his apartment, I called Tim on his cell. I asked if he checked out the two men who were working with Jim the morning of the murder. He said that neither of the men had a police record. He also told me that both men said that they were working right along with Jim Jamison at the time the murder was committed.

I asked Tim if he talked to the Ponzetti and Harris families about the morning of this murder. He said that both families said that they heard nothing unusual between six and nine.

I told Tim that someone must have heard that gunshot. I added, "All of these people can't be deaf. I don't think they want to get involved again." I told Tim that I would see him back at the station after I took a guided tour of Jim Jamison's two room apartment.

Tim said, "I'm on my way to this new pizza joint on the west side. Do you want me to bring you a slice or two back with me, for you? You're Italian. You must like pizza."

I told Tim that I was more interested in finding a murderer than eating pizza, and then I told him to bring me back two slices with pepperoni, sausage, anchovies, black peppers, and extra cheese.

When Tim questioned Celine Selsnick, Rena's co-worker, she said that Jim Jamison's apartment was a dump. She wasn't kidding. When I entered the apartment with Jim, he asked me if I wanted a beer. I told him no, because I was still on duty.

Jim got himself a beer. When he opened the refrigerator, I saw the little green boxes of candy Celine had spoken to Tim about. I asked Jim if I could have a piece of candy.

He said, "I have a box opened on the counter over

there. Take what's left in it."

That's exactly what I wanted. I wanted to have a box, just in case I needed to know what it looked like later on in my investigation.

Jim said, "I guess you know by now I used to bring Rena to this apartment."

I said, "Yes I know you brought her here, and I know you also brought Celine Selsnick here as well."

"That crazy bitch," Tim said. "She had a big mouth, and she is married. I didn't need a jealous husband coming after me."

"This guy talks out of both sides of his mouth," I thought to myself.

I tasted a piece of the candy. It was very good, and I asked Jim where he purchased the candy.

Jim said, "I order ten boxes at a time off the internet. It comes from a chocolate distributor in New York City. It's imported from France, so the candy is awfully expensive. I get a better price when I buy ten boxes." Jim then added, "I use the candy for services rendered, if you know what I mean, Pete."

I thought to myself again, "Boy is this guy a sleaze bag. It's a wonder he has a daughter who's wacky."

Jim said that he thought I should know that he owned a gun. I asked him what kind of gun and where was it? He told me that it was a .44 magnum and he stored it in his garage at his home. He added that he had a license for it.

I didn't see anything unusual at Jim's apartment. After all, I couldn't look around that much since I didn't have a warrant. I thanked Jim for the mini tour. As I was leaving, Jim looked at me with a serious look on his face and said, "Tell me Pete, do you know who may have killed Rena?"

"I thought you did," I fired back. "I thought you may have killed Rena in retaliation for her killing your son. I guess I was wrong, and I'm not usually wrong. My partner

Tim made a few calls, and your alibi checked out. Seem you couldn't have killed Rena."

I checked with the laptop in my car about Jim's gun license. The computer confirmed that Jim had a license for a .44 magnum for the past six years. Too bad he didn't own a 38.

Chapter XXIII

I looked up the number for Bruce Banton, Jamie's only close friend. A woman, or who I thought was a woman, answered my call. I said, "I'd like to speak to Bruce Banton."

The person on the other end of the line said, "Speaking."

I introduced myself, and then I asked Mr. Banton if I could question him about Rena's murder.

He said, "Can I refuse to talk to you?"

I said, "Sure you can, but then you'll have to come to the police station for questioning."

Mr. Banton told me that he would be waiting for me.

I arrived at Mr. Banton's home about forty minutes later. He answered the door and I couldn't believe it. He sounded even more feminine in person. Just between you and me, I think this kid's parents should have named him Bruella or Brucinda. I asked (I'll call him Bruce) where I could ask him some questions. He said that we could talk in the kitchen around a small counter.

Bruce was a squirmy looking little guy with greasy curly black hair. I'm pretty sure he was wearing make-up, or had some cream on his face to cover a bad complexion. I'm sort of leaning toward the make-up angle.

I asked Bruce if he knew Rena Renton. He told me he saw her a few times when he took Jamie to the library to pick up a paycheck for his Dad.

I asked Bruce if he ever met Jim Jamison. "I don't think I've ever met him," he answered.

I said, "Jamie was your close friend, and you never ran into Jamie's father at his house?"

"No, he was usually at his dingy apartment on the North Side," Bruce replied.

I said, "So you know about Jim Jamison's apartment on the North Side?"

Bruce said defensively, "Yes, I heard Jamie talk about it a few times."

I asked Bruce how he new it was dingy.

He said, "Jamie must have mentioned that as well."

I asked Bruce what he did for a living. He said that he was an aspiring writer.

I said, "Oh, a writer, huh? What do you write?"

"I've written a few murder mysteries. I currently have a few backers that are trying to get one of my stories published," he replied.

I thought to myself, "Yea, probably a few old backers that have a lot of money in exchange for something. Backers, get it?" I asked Bruce where he was Tuesday morning between the hours of six and nine.

He said, "I was here. I did leave my house once to go down the street and get some breakfast."

I asked Bruce the name of the restaurant, and asked if anybody would remember him being there.

He replied, "The name of the restaurant is JoJo's and I've only been there a few times. They were pretty crowded that morning and I don't think anyone would remember seeing me."

I asked Bruce if he remembered what his waitress looked like.

He answered, "No. All waitresses look the same to me."

That wasn't a very good answer. But then I thought about it for a moment. When the guy is a homosexual, he may not remember what a waitress looked like. If it was a cute male waiter he might. Then I asked him if he owned a pistol, specifically a .38 caliber one.

That really set him off. He said, "Whoa! Am I a suspect in Rena Renton's murder? Do I need a lawyer?"

I hate to hear that question, "Do I need a lawyer?"

"First of all, anyone related to this case has the potential of being a suspect. It all depends on their alibi, and you don't have a very good one." I added,

"You have the right to an attorney. You can obtain one, and we can continue this conversation at the police station."

Bruce told me that I could do the questioning there and he was waiving his attorney privilege.

I said, "Okay Bruce, do you own a .38 pistol?"

He said, "I don't own one, but had one that was stolen from me."

I asked Bruce if he reported that the gun was stolen.

He said, "I couldn't report it stolen because Jamie Jamison stole it from one of the offices that he cleaned."

I said, "So Jamie Jamison stole a gun for you. What did you need a gun for and where was it stolen from?"

Bruce said that the gun was stolen from him at Bally's Gym. He said that he received a temporary membership from a friend and went there to work out a few times.

I asked if he reported the theft of the .38 to the Bally's employees. He said that he didn't get around to it yet.

"You still didn't tell me why you needed a gun."

"I needed it for protection," he said.

I said, "Protection from what?"

Bruce said, "You see I'm gay, and straight guys tend to pick on gay guys. I just needed a gun if I encountered any threatening situations."

I thought to myself again, "He's gay. What a shock. I never would have guessed it."

As I was about to leave I spotted a couple green boxes of that imported candy. I asked Bruce if I could have a piece of it.

"You can have both boxes. I really don't like chocolate," he told me.

I told Bruce not to leave town because I would probably have some more questions for him at a later time.

This kid was starting to look good for Rena's murder. I still think that Jim Jamison is involved somehow. What I needed was a murder weapon. I decided to speak with Wynona and see if I could get search warrants for Bruce's house and automobile. I planned on letting Tim conduct these searches. I also wanted to get a search warrant for Jim Jamison's little hide-a-way; I had to get a better look at that place.

I stopped at the station to see Wynona. She said she would have warrants for me the next morning. I told Tim to get the search warrant for Bruce's home and automobile when he got to work the next day and that since Jim's apartment was small that I wanted to go search through it by myself.

The next morning, Wynona gave me the warrants. Tim had not arrived yet. If I know him, he probably stopped for breakfast. I was writing a note telling him to be as thorough as possible when searching Bruce Banton's home and vehicle. As I was writing Tim's note, he arrived. He said that he had slept in. I threw the note in the trash and told him what was on it and told him that we were getting close to solving Rena's murder.

Tim said that he was going to take a few uniformed officers with him to conduct his search of Bruce Banton's home. "We're leaving in a few minutes, but we have to stop for breakfast," he added.

I said, "Didn't those other guys eat already?"

Tim said, "Yes, but I didn't."

I arrived at Jim Jamison's home for the third time. I think if I set my GPS on his address the car would drive there automatically without needing assistance from me. I had to ring the bell three or four times until Jim answered.

He said that he'd worked all night, and that he was in bed sleeping. I showed him the warrant for searching his apartment. He said, "You've already searched my home.

What do you expect to find at my apartment? Besides that, you've already been to my apartment."

I said, "I know I've been to your apartment, but I didn't have a search warrant. When I go now I will have the authority to do a proper and thorough search." I told Jim that I had talked to Bruce Banton and that my men were currently searching his home and automobile.

"Bruce Banton, what the hell does he have to do with anything? He was just a close friend of Jamie's," Jim said.

I asked Jim if he ever met Bruce Banton.

He replied, "I saw him a few times with Jamie, but I was never introduced to him."

I told Jim that I saw a few green boxes of imported chocolate in Bruce's kitchen and that it was the same candy that I saw in his hide-a-way apartment.

Jim said that Jamie must have given the candy to Bruce.

I said, "Why would Jamie even have any candy. Your daughter told me that Jamie was a diabetic?"

Jim seemed very irritated and said, "You know, I really don't know, and I really don't care, and I'm going to tell you one thing: I'm going with you when you search my apartment."

I told Jim, "No you're not. Now give me the key to the apartment. You can wait here while I conduct my search or wait for me down at the station."

Jim knew I meant business and reluctantly handed me the key. I figured from our conversation that I'd better do a thorough search. It sounded like there was something in his apartment that Jim didn't want me to find.

I can't believe that the streets have not been salted. Thank God I have a four wheel drive vehicle. This snow is really getting on my nerves. I pay a small fortune in taxes to watch people almost slide into to me.

I called my father to find out what he was up to. I had failed to check the time when I made my call.

"What the hell is wrong with you," my father yelled. "Don't you know I'm watching my soap operas now?"

I apologized and told him that I was working on a difficult case and I forgot to check the time. I asked him to get out some ground meat out of the freezer when he got a chance and to have his stomach pills handy because I was going to make tomato sauce tonight.

I entered Jim's apartment to begin my search. I guess a little bit of Tim was rubbing off on me as I snitched a couple more pieces of that imported chocolate. Boy, that stuff was good.

After searching the apartment for an hour, we hadn't found a thing. I was sitting at a small table in the kitchen and was ready to give up on my search. I pride myself on my shiny black spade shoes. I looked down at them and saw a reflection of something under the table. I got down on the floor and looked up. I'll be dammed, what was this? There was a small computer disc taped under the table. This was something for our computer department.

I called Tim at Jim Jamison's and asked him how his search was going.

He said, "We're almost done and we haven't found anything yet. We still have to check out the front and back yards to see if anything has been buried recently."

I told Tim to check the warrant and make sure that it stated Mr. Banton's home and grounds. I didn't need another illegal search on our hands. Tim checked the warrant and said that it stated the home and grounds. I told Tim, just for the hell of it, to check under any tables in the kitchen for a small computer disc.

After a few minutes Tim said, "Are you a mind reader or what? I guess that's why they call you Columbo. There is a small computer disc taped under one of the tables."

I told Tim to bring the disc, and Bruce's laptop, to the station with him. I took Jim Jamison's laptop from his apartment. It will be interesting to see what are on these discs and laptops. Things were looking up, but I still don't have a murder weapon yet.

Chapter XXIV

Jack Remus was in charge of the computer department. Jill Poster was his assistant. Everyone at the department called them "Jack and Jill." They were actually an extension of our forensics department. The computer department really made a difference in how we checked our evidence now. They weren't CSI, but they were close. Tim and I dropped Jim Jamison's and Bruce Banton's laptops off along with the computer discs we'd discovered.

Jack told me to give he and Jill a couple of hours and they would probably have something for us. I took one of the boxes of the imported chocolate from Bruce's home that he gave me. I dropped them off at the forensics lab to be dusted for finger prints. I knew I could have these checked out because Bruce told me I could have them. I was working on a theory in my mind.

I decided to spend the next couple hours discussing the case with Tim. I wanted to start before his stomach gave him a food alert. We sat down in one of the interrogation rooms. I asked Tim who he thought may have murdered Rena Renton.

"Hey, you're the super cop. You tell me."

I blew that off and continued. "Jim Jamison has an excellent motive for killing Rena: revenge. Rena had murdered his only son. The only problem is that he has an iron clad alibi for the time of the murder. I don't know where Brucella fits in this case."

Jim said, "Who?"

Oh, I better watch myself. That's the name I gave myself for Bruce Banton. I better start calling him Bruce before I let that name slip out again.

Jim asked me why I would call Bruce "Brucella." I said "Didn't you notice anything about him?"

Tim said that he thought Bruce seemed a little girlish, but other than that he appeared to be a nice guy. I told Tim that Bruce was what the young people today call a flamer, a homosexual.

Tim looked at me with one of his classic stares and said, "Oh."

I continued, "Did I tell you that I found a box of that imported chocolate at Bruce's home? I just received a call from the forensics lab. They said the box contained two sets of prints, Jim Jamison's and Bruce's."

Tim said, "Obviously Jim Jamison's prints will be on the box. Didn't he pass them out to his sexual conquests as sort of a reward? And, if you took the box from Bruce's home his prints would be on it."

I told Tim, "I mentioned seeing a couple boxes of the chocolates at Bruce's home to Jim Jamison. Jim told me that Jamie probably gave them to Bruce. Why weren't Jamie's prints on the box if that's the case?"

Tim said that what I was saying didn't make a lot of sense. I told Tim that it would make a great deal of sense if my theory was right.

Tim said, "What theory?"

I said, "Here goes. The reason that Jamie's prints weren't on the box is because Jim Jamison gave the boxes to Bruce. I think that Jim Jamison is a switch hitter. I also think that he was having a homosexual affair with Jamie's friend Bruce, and was having a straight affair with Rena Renton. I don't know when this guy had time to work."

Tim said, "Boy, you never cease to amaze me! Where did you come up with a scenario like that?"

I replied, "We'll see if this scenario plays out when we see what's on those discs and laptops."

I asked Tim if he wanted to go with me when I went

to see Jack and Jill, or if he was only ready to stuff his face again. Tim said that he would hold off on getting something to eat. I was surprised. I think he wanted to see if my theory was right.

Chapter XXV

Jack looked a little embarrassed when Tim and I saw him. Jill's face was as red as a ripe tomato. I said, "I assume you two have found something."

Jack said, "First of all, the two discs are identical. They are computer cam movies of two men engaged in homosexual activities."

I asked Jack to show Tim and I a few minutes of one of the discs. Tim and I wanted to identify Jim Jamison and Bruce Banton on their homemade porno film. I asked Jack what else he had found on the laptops.

Jack told me that Jim Jamison's laptop indicated that he had visited a lot of porn sites, "Mostly straight sex porn," he said. Jack told me there were a few homosexual porn sites he viewed as well. Jack also saw invoices indicating that Jim Jamison ordered a lot of imported chocolate from a site in New York City. Jack added that Bruce Banton's laptop showed he only visited homosexual porn sites.

I asked if there were any murder mysteries on Bruce's computer, since he said that he was an aspiring writer.

He said, "No, why?"

I answered, "Bruce told me that he'd written a few murder mysteries, that's why."

Jack said, "Well, they're not on this laptop."

I looked at Tim and said, "Well, I told you, didn't I?"

Tim said, "Yes, you did. But what they were doing is not against any laws. This just proves that Jim Jamison and Bruce were lovers."

I told Tim that I wanted to check out Bruce's home again for a .38 pistol.

Tim said that he was getting hungry. He asked me if

I wanted to go to Max's for one of their huge sandwiches, and that it would be his treat. Since he was buying, the question hit a magic place in my brain. I agreed to go to lunch with him. I called the DA and told her I needed a rush search warrant for Bruce's apartment.

Oh my, what a mistake it turned out to be going to lunch with Tim. I'd never eaten with him before. It was hard enough for me getting my mouth around one of Max's sandwiches, but Tim had his own calculated way of doing it. He took little bites around the edge of the sandwich and let the excess fall to his plate. Then he would use his fingers to pick everything up and stuff it into his mouth. He managed to talk the entire time he was executing this disgusting eating maneuver. After a few minutes I couldn't watch him anymore. I told him that I had an upset stomach (which I honestly did at this point) and that I was going to take my sandwich home for my Father. I told Tim that I would wait for him in the front of the restaurant. It was cold and snowing outside, but I had to get away from him.

When we arrived back at the station, Wynona had another search warrant for Bruce Banton's home. I decided to take Tim with me.

Bruce greeted Tim and I at his door and wanted to know why we had returned. I told him that Tim and I decided that we needed to search his home again and that I didn't believe his story about the .38 being stolen. I also told him that we saw what was on the disc that was taped to the bottom of his table.

He said, "So? What Jim and I were doing isn't illegal."

I said, "You're right, but Jim Jamison told me he never met you. Why do you suppose he told me that?"

"I don't know," Bruce answered.

I told Bruce to have a seat because Tim and I would probably be there for a while. I was wrong.

I decided that Tim and I should conduct this search together. I also knew that when two people look at something, one of them may see something a little different. I looked over at the Living Room fireplace and observed fresh ashes. I felt them and they were still a little warm. I called Tim over and asked him if he remembered any ashes in the fireplace on his previous search.

Tim said, "You know it's funny that you should ask. When I saw the fireplace on my previous search I wondered why it looked like it was never used. With the temperatures in the teens the last few weeks, I figured that Bruce would have made a fire a few times."

I began to separate the ashes. I couldn't believe it. Under a grate in the fireplace was a .38 caliber pistol. I turned around to ask Bruce about the gun. He was not in the room. I told Tim that we better find him and for him to check downstairs while I checked the upstairs rooms. When I arrived at the top of the steps I immediately saw a stream of blood flowing on the floor out of the bottom of a room. I hollered for Tim to come upstairs. The door was locked, so I broke it down. Bruce was lying on the floor in a pool of blood. Tim had arrived by then and I told him to call the medics. After I looked at Bruce a little closer I told Tim to call the coroner instead. Bruce had slit his wrists and his throat as well. In the little bit of time that we looked for him, he had bled to death.

On the bed beside Bruce was a note. It read, "I'm sorry for killing Rena Renton. Jim Jamison paid me $5,000 to kill Mrs. Renton. I really needed the money, which that is why I killed her. Being gay, I didn't want to spend any time in prison."

Tim had scribbled his note in haste, but he had the hindsight to sign this suicide/confession note. This fact would have a great impact on arresting Jim Jamison for the murder of Rena Renton. I called the station and had several uniformed officers sent to Jamison's house to arrest him for murder.

Chapter XXVI

I entered the interrogation room and said hello to Jim Jamison. He was actually a little indignant towards me. He asked me why he was being charged with Rena's murder.

I said "Your boy toy gave you up. About an hour ago, Bruce Banton killed himself and left a suicide note. Fortunately for us, Bruce's note implicated you in Rena's murder. On his suicide note Bruce wrote that you paid him $5,000 to kill Rena Renton for him." I told Jim that we knew that he and Bruce were very close friends and we saw what was on their computer discs.

Jim said, "Well there's no law against that."

You know, I get awful tired of hearing that.

I said, "You know, that's exactly what Bruce said. I can tell you that there's no law against what you and Bruce were doing, but there is a law against murder for hire. I know you were read your rights. Do you want an attorney present while you give me your confession?"

"I'm not giving you a confession, hot dog," he blurted.

"I think you should," I said. "I have talked to the District Attorney and she said that if you are willing to cooperate she wouldn't seek the death penalty. Don't get me wrong, we have the murder weapon and plenty of evidence against you and Bruce, and we also have that suicide note implicating you."

I continued, "Bruce chose to cut his wrists and his throat rather than spend the rest of his life in prison. And I know this won't mean anything to you, but I think he really cared for you." This got no reaction from Jim, though I really didn't think it would.

I could tell my blood pressure was rising when I said,

"When I first met you I felt sorry for you because you lost your only son. I no longer feel that way, of course. I feel sorry for Jamie for having had such a rotten father. You have ruined so many lives: Rena's, Rena's husband Ed, and now Bruce. And I'm guessing that you caused your wife to drink herself to death. I'm happy to know that you will be going to the gas chamber for your murderous ways."

Jim said, "I think you have the penalty wrong there. First degree murder in this state carries a penalty of life without parole."

I replied, "I see you've done your homework, but you've not done it very well. First degree murder with extenuating circumstances carries a penalty of death by the gas chamber. The extenuating circumstance here is that you hired someone to commit murder for you." I added, "Enjoy the air that you breathe, because you won't be breathing it for much longer."

Chapter XXVII

I ran into Tim in the hall.

He said, "Well, we did it."

I guess he did help me on the case. "Yes we did Tim. Congratulations. Let's go to Max's and I'll buy you a sandwich." I was so happy that we got that bastard Jamison that I was willing to watch Tim eat another sandwich at Max's.

I can't believe Christmas is only two weeks away. Years ago my father didn't have the movie making technology that we have today. I knew that he has a huge box of old 8mm movie reels up in his closet. I heard of a place that transfers old movies on to CD's. I'm going to get my Father's old movies transferred to CD's for him as a Christmas present. He still has a great deal of his memory in tact.

Epilogue
Two Years Later

A lot has happened the past two years. My ex-partner
Tim quit the force after the Renton murder case. He took
a job in Chicago working in a high class restaurant. He
started out as a salad maker, but I heard the other day that
he has been promoted to assistant chef. Go Tim! I think he
made a wise decision.

Ed Renton retired and moved to his brother's home
in Florida. Celine Selsnick is now the head librarian at the
Claysville Library, and Patrick Ponzetti does odd jobs for
her. Wynona Williams ran for political office and is now a
State Representative. Sarah Stein lost her first case when
she defended Jim Jamison.

Speaking of Jim Jamison, he is currently on death row
in the Illinois State Correctional Institute. He did do one
unselfish thing in his life. He signed over his expensive
home on the West Side to his daughter Julie. Julie sold the
home and moved to the North Side with us common folk.
She successfully completed a drug rehab program and is
currently attending Illinois State University. And, by the
way, she dumped her loser boyfriend, Buster.

I'm glad I had my father's old movies made into CD's.
When I gave them to him, little did I know that it would
be his last Christmas. He died of a heart attack about three
months after that Christmas. He watched the CD's every
night, and I watched them at his side. I'm sure he took all
of those happy memories with him.

So, what has happened to my life in the past two years?
I started dating Janet, the waitress at Max's, a short time

after Jim Jamison's trial. We have been married now for over a year. I retired from the department and Janet and I recently passed our real estate exams. I continue to slide all over the streets of Claysville in the winter. They are still very lax in snow removal. Life is grand.

About the Author

After writing three books of poetry I finally admitted to myself that most people don't read poetry let alone the four-line end rhyme style that I write. I decided to write a book of short stories and this novel.

I realize that the years are moving on so I thought I'd take one more shot at writing. I quit drinking more than 25 years ago, and I have quit smoking over five years ago. I'm hoping to squeeze some additional years into my life span.

I really love to write. Besides spending time with my wife, there is nothing I would rather do with my time. (Oops, I forget bowling.)

I have grown as a writer since I published my first book in 2005. My time now will be spent promoting my two new books. I wrote this murder mystery to be included in my first book, but it was too long. So it ended up getting published by itsel, as you can see.

On occasion I also write made-to-order poetry for special occasions. This has proven to be an enjoyable side business for me. I've also written a few poems dedicated to my favorite city, Pittsburgh, PA. Some of those poems have found their way into my local newspaper.

I've spent my entire life in the city of Pittsburgh, Pa. There is no greater city in the world, and truthfully I feel sorry for people who don't live here. They don't know what they are missing. I believe that when I die I'll be leaving Pittsburgh, PA on earth and moving on to Pittsburgh, PA in heaven. My brother-in-law calls me the Pittsburgh Poet and, if that's true, it is an honor I carry with pride. Maybe I can add "The Short Story King" handle to that title.

So get yourself a cup of coffee or tea, no cigarettes

or alcohol please, and snuggle up in your favorite chair and enter into some creations from my mind.